A Gia

AJ Saxsma

First Edition

ISBN: 979-8-218-03812-0

CONTENTS

For you.

CHAPTER ONE

The boy had not slept. His father had paced the apartment and sang and laughed and kept the boy from sleep late into the night. Despite his heavy bones and tired head, the boy loaded his wooden cart with the day's parcels. The sun had not yet risen. The air was cold. His lungs were dry. His uniform was pressed, and his cheeks and fingernails washed with his father's good soap. He pulled his wagon onto the street while the other boys punched their timecards and smoked cigarettes and cleared the sleep from their eyes. Bands of morning stirred the young city, and the streets soon filled with sunken faces and shouting and movement. Greetings met the boy on his route, and he delivered his allotted parcels with decorum and gentleness.

His father, who was unemployed, had told the boy their forefathers delivered many letters and packages of great import for many kings of men to all corners of this and many lands. The boy had been honored to join in his family lineage.

By evening, his cart was empty and he returned to collect the day's earnings. A lumpy cloth sack waited for the boy. Inside were a half-dozen sweet peppers, a potato, and a slab of old beef.

'My stores have no room. They will spoil,' the supervisor said. Just the week prior, the supervisor had gifted the boy broth and other vegetables and had given the same excuse. 'They will spoil. My stores are full.' The week before that it was the same, 'They will spoil.'

The supervisor hid much pity for the boy; he had done it with such incredible frequency and so he pretended to work but instead watched the boy and ensured the bag went home with him.

The boy's father was laid across the couch when the boy entered the apartment. A newsboy screamed from the street that reports suggested another long winter. Flies buzzed atop food plates scattered about the boy's father, who promptly requested the boy's earnings and received them with no friction.

His father's breath stung the boy's eyes. His father filled a glass with warm liquid the color of honey and pocketed the money.

'I have taught you this reliability, no doubt, as my father taught me. Our blood is honest, my boy. Our blood can be counted on in dark days. We are of an incredibly dependable bloodline.'

The boy cooked the gifted peppers and meat with spices and chopped potato. A wonderful scent filled their small apartment and masked the slothful smells of his father. The boy would bathe him tomorrow.

He and his father ate and listened to the newsboy shout headlines. His father filled another glass. The boy went to bed and his father filled one more. Many dreams came to the boy but when he woke in the morning he remembered none of them.

The boy prepared a breakfast of leftover dinner and brewed coffee for his father.

'Smells good, boy,' his father grumbled.

He searched for the bottle.

'I am to trial in the factory today.'

'And if you do well?'

The boy's father found the bottle and emptied it into his coffee. 'They will ask me back. You and I shall leave this pit.'

The boy's spirits rose. Through the day, he believed his father and had visions of a home filled with laughter and much warmth. It would be a home of peace and stillness and there would be no troubles there and worry would be gone from there and there would be no screaming and hitting there. There would be no stinging words there.

After his route, the boy collected his wages.

'One moment,' the supervisor said. 'There is one more parcel. It came just an hour ago.'

The supervisor presented a package wrapped in clean and plain brown paper and tied snug with ribbon. The attached card read, For Dad.

'But the day is done,' the boy said.

'It is to reach its destination by morning.'

'My father needs help in the evenings. He's not well.'

'I am instructed to offer one hundred shillings for receipt of delivery, courtesy of the sender. I do not trust the others, they are lazy and greedy. You are my most reliable courier. None is more deserving.'

'One hundred shillings?'

The supervisor indicated inside his desk. 'Paid in advance.'

'For a common parcel?'

'The sender insisted I extend the offer.'

'I am to deliver it and no more?'

'This and no more.'

The boy thought and then he accepted. The supervisor would send word of his tardiness to the boy's father.

'You mean to tell him of the money?' the boy asked.

'Only if you wish.'

'I do not.'

The boy smoothed his uniform and rode his delivery cart over the bridge, there were no hungry and none with illness this side of the river. The roads were smooth and easy to ride and were coddled by tall, furry trees. Stately homes stood wide, crafted by the finest materials from the south and many held wondrous gardens full of vivid flowers.

The boy felt unwelcome.

A vast keep of sturdy stone and iron awaited the boy and the package.

The boy knocked, package in hand. He stood straight with his shoulders back and stiff. A rehearsed but no less honest smile appeared. He waited many long minutes, rigid in his form, then knocked once more. There was no answer.

A cold dark crowded the few windows, beyond which the boy could not see. The boy returned to the cart in disappointment. Then a man well into his winter years emerged. A hunch or injury caused him to lean forward, even when upright. A deep gash had healed into his neck, probably from his youth, and had not healed in a pleasant manner. It was composed of a strange shape. It unsettled the boy.

'Don't knock on my door.'

'You've a package, sir.'

'What?'

'I'm a courier. If you could sign, sir?'

A blood haze hung in the whites of the old man's eyes, much like the boy's father. The tips of his pillowy whiskers were dead and rusty and coiled. A shiver began in his wrist and did not stop.

'Must I accept?'

'I suppose no.'

'Then I do not want it.'

'But, sir, someone sends a gift and a card.'

'Certainly one gentleman or gentlelady in all the routes the world round has, before, declined delivery.'

Disappointment fell over the boy.

'I suppose so.'

The old man closed his door to the boy. The sun had nearly gone from the wide sky.

Activity withdrew from the streets and the boy found he was alone. He pulled the wagon home with a beaten color locked in his slouched frame, past the hushed doors and big windows and the glimmer of candlelight, past the black shadows of families joined together inside.

He would tell the supervisor of his failure in the morning.

* * *

The boy's aunt had come to tidy the apartment and see to his father. An argument, it seemed, had already begun and ended between his father and his aunt when the boy came in. They were not speaking to one another and were not near one another. Dinner had been prepared for the boy, but he was not hungry.

He retired to his bedroom.

His aunt entered. Her hair was draped across her cheeks and was dry and ratty from cleaning.

'You work too hard, boy.'

'Father says our men were nobles and that they couriered for royalty.'

'Your father's a damn fool.'

'He's not well.'

'That is his choice.'

'He will come around.'

'You're short of rent. The collector will allow no more favors.'

'Father manages the money.'

'He surely manages to spend it. You can drink a bottle but you cannot sleep under one.'

Her large body sat beside him.

'Stay with me. There is more room and food than one woman needs. You were my sister's only boy, which makes you mine.'

'Father says her hard time has ended and that his still persists. He says it is unfair. Father needs me.'

Her hand took the boy's and held tight. 'You care for him deeply. Your mother did, too.'

The boy nodded. 'He improves.'

His aunt drew a short breath and shook her head, saddened for the boy. 'You sound like her.'

'He trialed the factory today.'

'No. He returned to sleep and missed and the factory will no longer have him.' Her weight left the bed and drifted to the hall. 'I will not say what I said to your mother then, in the days before. It did not work. It won't now.'

The boy's aunt prepared her leave.

'Should you change your mind, lean from the window there and whistle and I will come and steal you from this pit.'

The boy bathed his father. The man's eyes were watery and distant and his words sounded as mush. The boy lay in bed, in the dark and until late in the night. His father had the radio up loud. The boy heard bottles and weeping.

The boy rose from bed but not to tend his father's suffering. He climbed down to the street from the window. The town slept like a corpse. In the deep of night, it felt abandoned.

He crossed the bridge and returned to the stately homes and, once more, knocked upon the old man's door. Sleep had not yet released the old man when he crooked his head out a window.

'Package, sir.'

'What's the hour?'

'We're very dedicated.'

'You've been told no once. Again won't be as pleasant.'

'Once in your possession, could you not do with the package as you please?'

'What?'

'I must do my job, sir.'

'Your job now is to take that package from my sight!'

'I will not!'

'Away!'

'The sender has promised one hundred shillings for delivery.'

'I would not accept that package from you if he promised one million.'

'My father needs it, sir.' The boy broke into tears and it caused an ugliness upon the old man's face.

'He relies on the wages of his boy?'

'Sir?'

'He's a pig? A sloth? A fat cow?'

The boy wept and the door soon opened to him.

'Come in, boy.'

The boy entered.

Many dozens of paintings were arranged through the old man's home. Frames of cherry wood and gold held mountain landscapes and lakes and far-off lands. One encased a beautiful village at dusk and it had been set apart from the others.

The boy wiped his tears and the old man led him to the kitchen and warmed two glasses of cow's milk. It soothed their bellies.

'Are you so cruel as to refuse the duty of a boy in need?' the boy asked.

'You would prefer to know why?'

'I would.'

'You would find satisfaction no other way?'

'I would not.'

The old man studied the boy and tapped his finger upon the table, then he poured a second milk for the both of them and warmed them at the fire.

'Then I shall tell you a story.'

The old man began his story...

CHAPTER TWO

A long time ago ...
The old man was, back then, just a young boy himself, far beyond the city and the valley, in a place most had forgotten, and he was walking down a dirt road through the fields clothed in rags.

His feet were black and swollen, but he did not notice. Heat hung in the air and he had a terrible thirst. A traveler on horseback approached. Behind him he pulled a riderless mustang with fur like autumn leaves. The mustang fought the traveler's draw with stubborn attitude.

'Boy?' the traveler said.

The boy looked up at him, into the bright sun. Offensive body odor drifted from the man. Grease, for lack of bath, shone in his dark hair, and his teeth needed a brush.

'Have you a father?'

'No.'

'A mother?'

'No.'

Concern rose on the traveler's dirty face. 'Have you food?'

'No.'

The traveler considered the road ahead.

'Can you ride?'

'Yes.'

The mustang calmed beneath the boy's touch. It rode swift as wildfire. By nightfall they had left the fields and followed the river to the purple mountains with sharp white crowns. The traveler began a fire and roasted two squirrels he had captured in the forest and boiled a head of cabbage.

The boy ate earnestly. The traveler was pleased. 'We make for the village north of here.'

The boy did not listen. He sucked animal fat from his fingers.

'I carry important news,' the traveler added.

The night shrank around their warm fire. Under a scratchy blanket, the boy curled and, with a glad belly, found sleep rather easily. The sun stirred first. Webs of steam rose from the grass and the trees and beams of sun turned them gold, like the halos of angels. They came to the village walls by midday. They were of stone and ran many miles. Guard towers stood as hollow statues, tall and silent and collecting shadow.

'Ho, there!' the traveler called up.

A small voice replied down, 'What?'

The traveler shouted all of this, 'Is this the village I'm told is home to the many gorgeous goods of the infamous Salt Creek Mercantile, the award-winning, full-bodied wines of the well-known Prairie Berry Brothers Winery, and the exquisite collected arts of the Madam Honeybrew Gallery?'

'It is.'

The boy tried but could not see from where on the wall the small voice came.

'I must speak with the village leaders at once.'

A small head poked from the wall, a small voice from a small head.

'You and every traveler before.'

'True, but they will, I am certain, be glad to have taken audience with me.'

'There's a waiting period.'

'What?'

'He said there's a waiting period.'

'I heard him. Quiet. Might the boy and I come in and rest our weary legs?'

'The waiting period is to get in.'

'That's absurd! How long's the wait?'

A basket lowered from the guard tower by rope. Inside were two parchment forms and ink and quill.

'What is this?'

'Registration. Tug the rope when you've finished.'

'This is most irregular!'

The man with the small head shouted down all of this, 'There's a filing period. Then thorough review. Approved applicant pools are submitted to the entry subcommittee, not the full, the sub. A preparatory hearing is scheduled, wherein they will schedule your first of three evaluation appearances before the entry full committee, that's full, not sub. After your third, you will file your formal Intent of Stay form, there's another review process, more appearances, and you will receive a decision through the post. Wait's four to five seasons.'

'The news I bring is urgent.'

'You need the escalation form.'

The basket rose and lowered again. Inside were the appropriate forms.

* * *

The traveler and the boy camped beneath the guard tower. It was cold; they were not allowed to make fire near the wall. Villagers came and went through the gate as they pleased. They were loud and ignored the traveler and the boy. A line of foreigners formed behind the traveler and the boy and waited for their application process to commence. The small-headed man came down the next morning. His legs were small, like his voice and his head. He informed the traveler and the boy their escalation forms had been approved.

They were taken to the village hall, a building of fine wood with bones of strong limestone. Outside, a shepherd guided his sheep through the street. He shouted at them and swatted them with his staff. The village leaders collected for the traveler and the boy. In attendance were the priest, the head merchant, and the head of the village watchmen. Age had beaten all three into wrinkled lumps. They were white as ghosts, and one would easily be mistaken for the other if not for their clothes and robes. They sat in thrones that were not thrones at all, in fact. The day's brightest sunlight climbed through the windows. 'I bring ill news,' the traveler said.

'What news?'

'A giant comes in three weeks' time. It will destroy the village.' The traveler humored the horse-laughter that followed.

'Bring the elder,' the priest said. Delighted tears of humor ran down his cheeks. 'He should share in our laughter.'

A watchman retrieved the elder. Long, clean robes lay down his frame. He was young, perhaps only a handful of years older than the boy. The elder rubbed sleep from his eyes and asked why his nap had been disturbed. The priest urged, 'Speak your news, traveler, exactly as you have toward us.'

'A giant comes.'

The elder looked to the leaders to confirm what he'd heard. 'It will arrive in three weeks' time,' the traveler added. The leaders erupted in laughter once more. The elder did not.

'Silence, fossils!' the traveler shouted. The leaders took great insult but obeyed. 'Due to your complex and absurd entry process, we have already lost one day,' the traveler said.

'A giant? You know this for certain?' the elder said.

'Our paths crossed when I was but a babe. It left nothing, save me. We met again, some years ago. I've spent this life hunting the monster. Now it travels the valley, heading this way.'

'It is well known I do fear giants,' the elder said.

'You don't say?'

'You hunt giants?'

'Just this one.'

'Our village watchmen are strong and brave and capable,' the elder said.

'Capable in the matters of men, surely, but those of giants? I tell you it cares not for bravery.'

'This is madness,' the leaders said. They closed on the elder and tugged his shirt for attention.

The elder waved them away. 'You bring this news, traveler. What would you have us do?'

'I would have you prepared to fight.'

The leaders voiced their discord with a moan. 'We are civilized people, simple and God-fearing farmers and smiths and laborers,' they said. 'We are no warriors.'

'Call for volunteers. With a wage and roof, I shall learn them to combat the giant and you shall have a formidable band.'

'Just how violent is this particular giant?' the elder asked.

'Terribly,' the traveler said.

'Then I shall decree it, a band of volunteers will be formed. Leaders, make note.'

'Apologies,' the traveler said. 'I meant to say with a substantial wage. Leaders, make note.'

The leaders assailed the elder with questions and disagreements. The elder quitted them and said, 'And the boy?'

'My son.' The traveler placed a hand on the boy's shoulder to halt his coming questions.

'The mother?'

The traveler saddened. 'Taken by the giant.'

* * *

Wild eggs and bacon and buttered bread rolls were brought for the traveler and the boy's hungry bellies. They were left to breakfast in peace. The traveler broke a foul herb into his water and drank it up. On the boy's queer look, he said, 'My remedies. I've need for more. Eat your fill, then I shall send you to identify the apothecary who tends this village's sick. Tell him I shall come tomorrow afternoon.'

The boy went when he could eat no more.

That evening, the elder shared the traveler's warning before all the village, and fear colored the people's eyes and they drew their children close and quaked and listened. Alongside the traveler and the boy, the elder made his decree. He said, 'Tomorrow we form a volunteer guard whose job it shall be to defend this commonplace village from the giant that comes. All are free to volunteer and will be forgiven all prior responsibility, to include field or trade work or employment, if accepted. The guardhouse will be cleared overnight and there the traveler will learn you to best the coming nightmare.' The traveler whispered in the elder's ear. The elder added, 'I'm told donations of food and coin are most welcome and strongly encouraged.'

Boos and hisses and protest broke from the merchants who had gathered. 'You cannot have our employees! Our businesses will suffer!' they shouted. Without haste, village watchmen removed them at the elder's request.

The traveler stepped forth. He said, 'It is terrible news I bring.' He allowed a moment of peace then said, 'I'm told questions help in processing.'

The villagers who remained began questions.

'Is the giant with club? Axe?'

'The giant wields both,' the traveler said.

The crowd shivered, and worry spread through its form. 'From where did it acquire arms?'

'Wherever giants acquire such things, of course. Next question.'

'Does it have one eye? Does it have a cock? How big's the cock?' The crowd demanded to know.

'Thank you. That'll be enough questions.'

The traveler ushered the boy away. Dusk spread its cold fingers, and guards lit torches through the streets. Unease hung over the village. The traveler and the boy were quartered in an unused guard's post near the stables, along the village's stone wall as the elder had decreed. They each made a bed of reeds and rushes and heavy wool blankets and lay to sleep. The floors stunk of urine and barley. The traveler rolled over, as if he'd just remembered. 'Does the apothecary expect me?'

'She does.'

Stillness returned to the room. The boy could not sleep. He spoke into the dark. 'I am to be your son then?'

'Do fathers not ensure their sons are fed and with roof o'er their head?'

'But could I not be the boy you found on the road?'

'There is a game all men play. We call it politics. It is better that you're my son, even just in word, than a boy from the road. If you cannot understand then I cannot explain.'

'And you've seen the giant you speak of?'

'I have. You will sleep now.'

They attempted sleep. Soon they found it.

CHAPTER THREE

The boy cleared the post's hearth of soot and dead leaves and began a fire for coffee. The room filled with its warmth.

It was ready when the traveler awoke with a moan and a mumble of words and questions aimed at the boy to confirm their whereabouts, as if he distrusted his own memory of events from the previous day.

Villagers ready to volunteer wrapped through the streets beneath the blanket of dawn in a terrible and unshapely line. Other villagers had set up tables and offered coffee and pastries to those in wait as thanks.

'A beautiful sight,' the traveler said in awe. 'Appeal to people's good sense, and they will surprise you, often pleasantly.'

The boy poured coffee. He sat by the window and looked upon the shapes standing in the early and cold dark. The men and women huddled and warmed their hands and swayed and spit. Not a word passed between them.

'Fear stirred them this morning. You scared them with threats of what comes.'

The traveler said, 'In the span of a single day, these men fear famine when crops die or when the soil sours as it does in the valley and they fear disease brought by wayward travelers such as we that may bring some to suffer the sweats and chills and which might lay some in the cold earth and they fear poverty from mounting debts and the burden of placing food in their family's bellies and roofs above their heads to shelter them as they sleep and live their days. They fear their love for others is not returned and they fear their incompetence, infidelity, and they fear the time that comes slow and then leaves swift. They fear life is more labor than joy, and joy is labor, and they fear all that is unknown. I say a giant does come and they have no fear left to bargain. It is brotherhood and nothing else that fills the hearts of these men and women who wait to serve our plight.'

'Men commit horrors in brotherhood.'

'Your youth's misfortunes curse you with a black judgment.'

'I spoke of no misfortunes.'

22

'An orphan boy wandering the road alone need not. They follow him unseen and they do color him with their fire.'

The boy softened and gently said, 'My father read me many books from his great library and taught me many lessons he gathered on his travels in the east, where men's skin is a different color and where they speak not of God and His glories but of peace and of self and harmony. He hoped to teach the savage men of these lands all he'd learned. They were not ready for it.'

'You have a father then.'

'No longer.'

'I stand firm, your judgment is black indeed.'

The traveler peered among the villagers and said, 'These men and women are virtuous, you will see.'

The traveler said no more and unpacked rolled parchment and ink from his bag. Inside the boy saw other items that the traveler obscured from his view. 'Take these items and this table outside. We must inspect our flock, we've no room for the inadequate in our band of giant killers.'

The crowd of waiting volunteers watched the boy place the table and two chairs out into the morning. The ground was still wet with dew and it was cold. The traveler exited the guard post and paraded to the table where he carefully placed instruments of strange design and unknown purpose. He read the men before him and they waited many moments for him to speak. Then the traveler stood upon a chair, his expression blank as stone, and, finally, he said, 'We shall begin evaluations. If a request strikes you odd, please understand that in the established and complex business of gigantic encounters, there are many oddities. The process and procedures you will see today are strictly regulated and certified of current code. Supporting paperwork for all of my gigantic claims is unavailable, unfortunately, due to fire, so you'll just have to take my word for it. If you are not selected, we thank you but you must leave. Please form a single line.'

A line was formed, though not straight. Heads poked out for a glimpse further ahead. This caused others to further their lean, and so on.

'It will get no straighter,' the boy said.

'I see that.'

The traveler seated, then the boy.

'Appraise with a keen eye,' the traveler instructed. 'Qualities we seek will be apparent almost from first sight.'

'What qualities do we seek?'

'Oh, many qualities, so many I don't think I could say. When in doubt, refer to me.'

The traveler waved the first volunteer over. He was a pallid man, a thin and sad thing withered by hunger. His bones were well displayed beneath his paper skin and his lips bore dried sores.

The starved man sniffled and did not smile.

'Welcome to our merry band,' the traveler said, and it was done. The starved man scrawled his name onto the traveler's record, then sat in the grass in wait.

'That starved man exhibited the qualities we seek?'

'Was it not plain to you?'

'I should say not.'

'Well, that is why I'm in charge.'

'You did not question him.'

'I needn't.'

'He is starved, a beggar most probably.'

'I am no judge of men's stations,' the traveler said. 'May we continue?'

The next volunteer in line approached. His tunic bore the mark of the village watchmen. He was tall with arms and shoulders hardened by numerous conflicts. His face bore scars which intimidated. His sword and sheath were maintained with great care.

'Study this one carefully,' the traveler whispered to the boy. The traveler eyed the man with suspicion. 'What qualifications have you?'

'For years I protected the lord whose lands lie to the west, along the shores of the great sea. He had not one complaint. A family quarrel robbed him of his estate and I joined this village's militia. Bandit raiding has since ceased, they know me far and wide and they do fear me. My sword skills are unmatched, and I can fell a tree with three swings of the axe. My militia brothers wrote letters of recommendation.'

Four letters on quality parchment were taken from his sack and gifted to the boy. They were sealed by ornate wax crests.

'Would you demonstrate your sword?' the boy asked.

The man drew his sword. It was a clean blade and sharp as wolves' teeth. A fine leather wrapped the hilt tight and it was hemmed in gold and, though the sword's weight was considerable, the man took a firm and defensive stance with grace and discipline. Without warning, he drove the idle blade through the morning air and carved from one fictitious opponent to the next. His body flowed with swift strikes in a fluid dance then went still in a feat of wondrous control.

He sheathed his sword and the villagers showered applause upon him.

Aside, the boy said, 'He holds great strength and appears quite able.'

'His sword is a blur in his hands!'

'Then we're in agreement?'

'Indeed.' The traveler showed the man a bright smile and said, 'We thank you, but no. Please leave the line.'

Foul words left the able man's mouth, promises of reprisals and insults. It left him short of breath, and then he stormed off.

'I don't think we were in agreement,' the boy said.

'A man filled with anger has no place in our guard.'

'But a man with anger has a thirst to fight.'

'Precisely! Next, please.'

The boy grumbled, and a woman stepped forth in a man's clothes. She had hair the color of dried wheat, which needed a long and thorough wash, and the boots on her feet were more empty than full.

'I am but a simple baker. I know not the ways of swordplay. I am a good and quick study,' she said. Her eyes carried a long, bereaved look and were quite fragile in appearance. She said, 'Would you permit a woman into your guard?'

'You will have no quarrel from me, unless the boy takes issue.'

'A woman's burdens build a back stronger than any man's, you understand,' she told the boy. In the boy's silence, she was quick to add, 'None will work harder than I.'

A grizzled look wrung the woman's face, and she leaned at the boy. Smells of flour and labor in the bakery fell on him. Similar smells would follow the boy's mother after a day of kneading dough and baking bread. The blankets of her bed would keep the scent. What came to him next were unpleasant images—the roar of a tall and sweeping fire, the struggle of binding rope, and smoke pillars rising into a darkened sky. Neither the traveler nor the woman noticed the disquiet in the boy.

'I take no issue,' the boy said.

'You will hold nothing back on my account, I demand it. I have toughed many struggles.'

'That I can promise,' the traveler said.

The woman joined the starved man in the grass and made known her name and the limitless nature of her brawn. Blades of grass poked from the starved man's mouth. He'd been eating it.

Face after face appeared before the traveler and the boy. They were old and young and freshly washed and there were those whose last bath was not known. They were eager and they were bored and there were those who simply sought forgiveness from work and trade as the elder had promised. By afternoon, the traveler had some fifty men and one woman ready to best the giant that he reminded them would soon come. The traveler stood before them. There were coughs and sneezes and whispers. Their sad and homely shapes pleased him, and nor did their unsavory habits displease him; nose and ear picking, crotch scratching and sniffing, blowing of noses onto clothing.

'Has there ever been a lot such as we, and as brave?' he asked the soiled crowd.

A cheer arose from the men and women then came to a peculiar silence. From the village center, a father and his small boy trotted their hungry mule down the road. A message had been painted, quite sloppily, into the mule's dark and coarse fur. It read "No Gyant Comes, Only Teerany!" A second mule, this one led by a tired young woman, followed the first. Her sign read "Bak to wurk!" Both parties were locked in an infantile and angry chant.

'Good Lord,' the traveler said, 'is there no village tutor?'

CHAPTER FOUR

The apothecary smelled of pumpkin and cacao and grain, but, too, of sweat and ripeness of body. Many times the traveler turned his head for relief from the strong odor. The boy stood near the window, which was open. Long shelves of jarred herbs and powders and dark liquids rattled while the apothecary, a dried crone in stained robes, moved about her collection.

'Yours is a rare remedy,' she said. 'What is your ailment?'

'I will not say,' the traveler said.

'You will not say?'

'Health is a private matter.'

'She means to help. Detail will only improve her ability.'

'I'm not here for inquiry or diagnosis.'

'I was only curious,' the apothecary said.

But the boy wasn't finished. 'Context is important in her study. That is for your safety,' he said.

'And for prying ears.'

'Have you not heard of the man who ingests a peanut and who then suffers a reaction of the body?' the boy asked.

'I have.'

'And his remedies must be free of the peanut.'

'Surely.'

'Then you would agree that a question which discovers this affliction, or any like it, has value?'

'I would not,' the traveler said.

'You would not?'

'I would not agree. Write the abbey to the north, high in the old mountains, if you must pry and know my personal matters,' the traveler said to the boy. He then asked the apothecary, 'Have you what I need?'

'I do,' the apothecary said. 'In plentiful supply.'

'I will take what will fit in this pouch.' The traveler offered his small leather pouch.

'I will not fill that pouch,' she said.

'You will not?'

'I am not to do business with you,' she said.

'You are not to do business with a customer?'

'I am not to do business with a customer who is you.'

'What have I done?' the traveler said.

'I haven't a clue,' she said, 'but you've upset them.'

The apothecary pointed outside to a long string of lively villagers who shuffled through the street, led by the father-and-son pair and their mule. No Gyant Comes, Only Teerany! They chanted to those who came from their homes and businesses to watch and to listen. The apothecary continued, 'They've had words with shops across the village. They are of the merchant guild, and none have more influence, save the church.'

The traveler fished for coins to give the boy and said, 'Pay the woman and let's be off.'

'The boy neither, he is an agent of yours and does your will. They were quite clear on that.'

'I found him walking the road! That he followed cannot be helped.'

'He promised food,' the boy corrected.

'I'm afraid no one will sell to you. The matter is done,' the apothecary said. She opened the door for the traveler and the boy to exit and waited for them to do so.

'I see.' The traveler's mind drifted in brief thought that seemed to the boy full of worry, or calculation, then he said, 'Good day.'

He took the boy by the hand and pulled him out into the street. 'Gather the volunteers this evening.

My tutelage must begin at once. I fear the giant closes in as we speak.'

'You said the giant comes in three weeks' time.'

'You heard wrong.'

'I'm certain I have not.'

'He comes in one week. I will not hear otherwise.'

The boy left to spread word.

* * *

The boy and the traveler spent the afternoon adapting the old post into a more comfortable and more permanent quarter. The boy swept the floorboards and cleared cobwebs. Lavish and costly rugs and pillows were donated by a volunteer skilled in the trade of textiles, to hide unsightly evidence of the post's age and to satisfy the traveler's extravagant tastes.

That evening, the boy collected the volunteers in the courtyard parallel the abandoned guard post. With mud, a giant was drawn in thick smears onto the village's perimeter wall some twenty feet high. It was in front of this crude and poor depiction the traveler began his first lesson.

'The first trait one must understand of the giant—'

The starved man aimed a string-finger at the mud illustration with disappointment. 'That's not very tall and therefore not discomfiting.'

'He's right, that isn't scary,' another villager said. A grumble of agreement traveled the crowd.

The traveler ignored him. 'The first trait one must understand of the giant is—'

Another villager said, 'He expects us to fear that?' Laughter spread. Volunteers departed the crowd.

Under their boisterous and heckling laughter, the traveler waved his arms for peace and stillness and was quick to say, 'Of course this isn't scary. If I were to accurately depict a giant before you, who've ne'er seen such a horror, why, I'm afraid your stomachs would twist into knots and your morning meal would reappear before our very eyes. Some might even run home in great fear and not return. Would this be an effective introduction to our foe?'

This made sense to the crowd, and its many faces nodded. Those who had departed returned.

'And this very observant villager is right, good eye on you, it is not very tall, is it? Heheh. A real giant stands many buildings high, and this wall, meant to keep out bandits and invaders, the real giant would simply step over without issue. You are right to jest at the giant's likeness, but the real one who makes for this village will turn your blood cold. He was born from the land while the Lord's creatures were yet crawling the dirt of His creation. Your village is but a small animal to him, easily snuffed from existence. He brought ruin to my village, to my home, together we must spare yours this terrible fate.'

From their silence and attentiveness, the boy, who had witnessed the traveler's words instill worry and then replace it with hope, knew the crowd was pliable once more.

The traveler knew it too.

'May I proceed?' the traveler asked.

There were no rebuttals.

'Once more, the first trait one must understand of the giant is—'

'Shouldn't we have weapons?' the woman said.

The crowd agreed.

'Probably. No more interruptions, please.'

He waited to begin. None from the crowd caused further interruption.

'The first trait one must understand of the giant—'

'Pardon this second interruption,' the starved man said.

The traveler hid his annoyance and said, 'Yes?'

'When is dinner?'

The crowd echoed the question and it circulated and they grew distracted over the matter.

The traveler contemplated then admitted, 'I could eat.'

* * *

After a decadent feast offered freely to the boy, the traveler, and the volunteer guard by supportive and servile villagers, the elder hosted a celebration in the village square to honor the volunteers' bravery and sacrifice. Families contributed sweets and cakes and children ran and shoved one another for amusement. Musicians sang old and new songs and played joyful music, and the villagers danced and released their burdens, and they drank wine and ale and grew full in stomach and light in heart and also in modesty. The sun laid to sleep and stars awoke and the village became cold and dark. A great fire was made and brought to life, a fire that swelled and loosed thick smears of smoke across the square. Firelight leapt about the excited droves and died in the shadows. Laughter rose into the night.

The priest chose not to attend for reasons of the shepherd, but his flock were among the first to fill their cups and stuff their mouths, even before the volunteers. Sloppy laughter engrossed them and they spilled their drinks and toppled here and there. Their hands were swift and searched one another to uncommon and inappropriate lengths. Some left in pairs, and not always with whom they'd come.

The traveler drank and ate himself into lethargy and the boy watched in silence from the edge of the firelight, where he was alone. A young girl sat beside him and began small conversation.

He moved away while she talked.

Many hours went by. The crowds thinned and the village and then the square fell to stillness.

Bodies lay in the street, drunken and comatose. Near the fire, where homeless villagers had gathered and kept close and held their hands to the flame, the woman sat beside the boy, but he did not move. He thought she resembled his mother.

Firelight avoided her eyes and left them black. She took large swills of wine. Her consumption had passed levity and entered silent lament. Wine ran down the woman's chin and ran down her trousers, which were men's trousers. Her shirt, which was also a man's shirt, was loose. Old bruises along her neck and shoulders were visible.

She caught the boy looking and concealed them. He did not inquire. Minutes passed, and she could not help but say, 'Have you no curiosity, boy?'

'I am curious of things.'

'Of what things?'

'Heaven.'

'Of what awaits you?'

'I do not wish to go there,' he said.

'All wish to go there.'

'Not me.'

A heavy silence settled.

The woman, again, could not help but say, 'You hold no curiosity for the bruises of a woman?'

'Those are not curious to me.'

'They are curious to everyone in this village. They cannot help but blurt and ask. You did not.'

'Women in my village hid their bruises too. Their men were quick with excuses. They did not need them; we knew their origin.'

'Accidents are the origin of mine.'

'The women were good liars too.'

The great fire dwindled to dark wood and bright ash. The woman then, with sadness, said, 'Was there reprimand for their men?'

'No.'

The traveler stumbled to the fire. His lips and chin were stained with wine and he could not keep upright. His face was apple red and warm without help from the fire. A group of merchants approached him and demanded the volunteer guard disband and that their workers return. Gold hung from their necks and they wore large rings and fine silks. Their bellies were round and full and bulging. Their legs and arms were softened by leisure and had no evidence of day labor. Incoherent sentences came from the traveler. The words the merchants could decipher were explicit insults that enraged them. They shouted threats and shoved the traveler who received their anger and who then vomited on their expensive shoes and drunkenly laughed into their shocked and upturned faces. They kicked him into submission then kicked and beat him more. The woman drew her sword. She stepped in and yelled, 'Away, miserly pigs!'

'We will not leave.'

'My sword insists.'

The merchants turned their anger on the woman. 'Our businesses suffer!'

'Your businesses deserve it!'

'Stories of you spread, woman. They tell of your unruliness to your employer, the baker, and the bakery's back room in the night hours.' Pig laughter burst from them. 'He waits for you to quit and return to work and to stop this nonsense, you cannot run, you cannot go, he waits.'

The woman swung the blade at the merchants. They toppled over one another in fright then fled and the woman chased them, waving the sword in threat and barking curses. The merchants' pleas for the watchmen went unnoticed; the watchmen were drunk and blacked out.

Both parties' screams faded.

CHAPTER FIVE

The traveler's sleep was shallow as drink had worn off and pain had set in. He woke before the sun with a groan and rolled over. He was back to sleep within a moment, and then woke again well after the sun had risen. He could not return to sleep; his body refused.

He rose and found the boy kneeled on the stone floor in the post's undercroft. His eyes were closed and his hands flat.

The boy repeated a mantra.

'What are you doing?' the traveler inquired.

'The hum you hear is a chant.'

'The sound is pleasant.'

'It means hail to the jewel in the lotus and is meant to calm and allay fears. My father learned this and others from monks in the east and wrote many books. He taught it to me, my mother, and my sister.'

'Why do you practice in the cold and the dark?'

'The church brands practitioners as blasphemers. They burn them at the stake. I've seen it.'

'May I sit and listen?'

The boy agreed and began again. The chants flowed from the boy's throat like water and were monotone, and his rhythm was uniform and full and dependable. Hidden in the boy's chanting was a hum that vibrated the boy's throat. It soothed the traveler and brought peace to the room.

'You will turn me in?' the boy asked.

'You've done no wrong in my eyes. Remove your guilt over the matter at once.' The boy stood with some strain and the traveler added, 'And for heaven's sake, lay a soft surface before your noise-making or you'll ruin your knees.'

The boy prepared a greasy breakfast and served it with hot coffee.

'Last night's festivities were wonderful fun, yes?' the traveler said. He tested pain in his knee and then his elbows. 'Good food, good drink.'

The boy did not agree.

'Why am I bruised and in ache?'

'Merchants accosted you.'

'A terrible taste lingers in my mouth.'

'You threw up on them.'

'I see.'

The traveler ate while his head throbbed.

'Report the merchants to the elder,' the boy said.

'No, I won't do that.'

'They're unlikely to relent.'

'Men of luxury, entrepreneurs, and the successful need to feel heard. They will calm.'

'The woman chased them away with a sword.'

'This usually happens. They will calm.'

'What usually happens?'

The traveler ignored the boy.

'You have done this before?'

'No.'

'You said, just now.'

'You misheard.'

'Saying that doesn't make it so,' the boy said.

'Yes, it does.'

'Then I have flown around the moon,' the boy said. 'Disprove me.'

The traveler rose with a turn of subject and said, 'I've decided we should report the merchants to the elder.' He washed his face and rinsed his mouth and with the boy crossed to the village hall. Outside, a crowd had gathered. The source of their interest was hidden behind their large number. Villagers spread for the traveler and the boy and made for them a path. They emerged at the front where a regiment of armored watchmen were atop strong steeds, and their wives and children were bidding them farewell. The wives wept. Cheers of pride rose from the children and they sang songs for the militia men.

Merchants exited the village hall and unto the crowds they said, 'True courage charges toward calamity. It does not sit and wait for its arrival.' The villagers agreed and applauded. 'These valiant watchmen ride for the giant it is said comes through the valley. They will do battle and fell the wicked creature and return heroes, and our commonplace lives will continue.'

Once more, the crowd voiced their agreement in volume and applauded. Some threw roses.

The merchants quickly added, 'Then the workers will return to work.' They skittered away like insects.

'Oh dear,' the traveler said.

The watchmen readied to depart, but the traveler stepped in their path. A painful smile was on his face. He said, 'I must insist you do not ride on, good men.'

A watchman strode nearer the traveler. He rode a large black steed with hair slick as oil. From within his steel helm he said, 'Brothers, the traveler begs.'

A good laugh spread among the watchmen.

'Brothers, I did not beg.'

'Remove yourself from our path.'

'I cannot.'

'Remove him against his will.'

A pair of watchmen approached the traveler. He stayed them with his hands and said, 'The giant is too dangerous to approach. You are not learned in their way, like me.'

'We do not shy from danger's cold eye.'

The traveler fumbled his words and began to sweat profusely. He stubbornly said, 'You do not know the giant's precise location.'

'It will be difficult to miss a giant in the valley.'

'Unless it is skilled in hiding.'

Watchmen and villagers and the boy waited for the watchman's next argument, but it did not come. Instead, he removed his steel helm. Beneath was the swordsman the traveler had turned down. He bore a sharp sneer and held his nose high. 'The merchants said you would speak your evasions upon us.'

'I wouldn't call them evasions.'

The watchman trotted forth his large steed and with a warm breath spoke into the traveler's face. He said, 'One might think you have something to hide.'

The traveler assured those within earshot he had absolutely nothing to hide.

The watchman donned his helm once more. 'Ride now, brothers!' He sounded a wild and violent battle cry, and the watchmen charged onward.

'Brothers, do not ride now!' the traveler said, but he was forced from their path and none heard. His protest was swallowed in whole by the swell of horses galloping and the cheers of the villagers and the roar of the watchmen. The dust settled and the crowds dispersed. The traveler stood with the boy.

They were left to watch the watchmen ride free of the village and climb the yellow hills beyond. When all trace of horses and men had gone and the land was quiet again, the traveler said, 'Their return shall prove interesting.'

'What makes you say this?'

The traveler continued staring into the hills. 'No reason.'

Sunlight warmed the streets.

The priest greeted the traveler and not the boy. He wore clean white robes and his pale hands were tucked into the long, flowing sleeves. He said, 'This morning I baptized many many godless and damned children, so many, I say, and while I lifted them into His love with my own hands, a thought came from the Lord direct, and it made known to me perhaps you and I started in an unbecoming manner.'

'Perhaps,' the traveler said.

'You all laughed when given news of the giant that comes,' the boy said.

'A small giggle,' the priest corrected.

'Your laughter filled the hall.'

'It is a large hall; echoes pass easily.'

'You decried the elder's decision,' the boy said.

The priest gave no more acknowledgment to the boy. 'Would you join me for lunch?'

'He has lessons with the volunteer guard,' the boy said.

'They will wait. I accept,' the traveler said.

The priest led the traveler to the church. When he noticed the boy following, he said, 'What are you doing?'

'He will join us,' the traveler said.

'Have you formalwear for the house of the Lord?'

The boy peered at his own tattered clothing. He was reluctant to answer.

'Of course, you don't,' the priest said.

He then led them into his church and through the nave where many rows of pews of a dark and strong wood crossed and where marble floors and columns thick as trees kept their gloss as though they were new and where hand-dipped candelabras of bright silver and ornate design hung from sturdy chains above their heads.

Frescoes spread along the walls and characterized God over Man, casting His judgment and raining His angels with sword and spear upon the Earth and rising from the lake of fire His demons to maim and rape Man and to steal him away to Satan's kingdom.

The artistry arrested the traveler where he stood, while the priest took the boy behind the sacristy to a store closet and told him, 'You will eat in here.'

'There is no table or chair.'

'One will be brought,' the priest said. 'In with you.'

The boy stepped in. 'There is no light.'

'My church is full of His light.'

The priest shut the door then showed the traveler through the kitchen, where congregants prepared a feast and cleaned the kitchen walls and floors and laundered the priest's robes and undergarments, and into the dining hall. A great table of dark and red oak had been set for two.

Both the traveler's and the priest's hands were wiped with cloth and dried and then they were seated opposite one another. Sun came in through stained-glass windows and filled the hall with magnificent color. Wine was served, along with fresh and assorted breads and warm soups. The priest sucked down the wine and the soups and ripped through bread with his teeth and he chewed while wine slipped from his lips.

Between bites and slurps and more wine he said to the traveler, 'The church I have built is said to be exquisite. Would you not agree?'

The traveler, who had not yet touched his food or drink, said, 'Truly.'

'The Lord protects our gracious halls from all our foes, be that man or giant.'

The smack of the priest's lips echoed.

The traveler said, 'You're certain?'

'I have faith.'

Congregants brought the priest more bread and refilled his chalice and replaced his soiled napkin with one that was clean and pressed. He did not thank them.

'Are you saved, traveler?'

The traveler choked on his wine. It spilled across his napkin. 'Sorry?'

'I said, have you accepted the Lord God into your dark sinner's heart?'

'My heart is plenty full.'

'Shall I save you?'

'That's all right, thank you.'

Congregants took the remaining bread and soups and served a stuffed peacock that had been roasted over an open fire. They plated for the priest first. He ate with his hands, and with grease on his chin he said, 'A trend began the day of your arrival. Sermons which were full in attendance are now sparse. This morning, none attended.'

'They missed a wonderful preaching to, surely.'

'You will have your volunteer guard answer their Holy duty, starting with this evening's service. With that, the matter is settled.'

'No, the matter is not settled. Responsibilities are in place. They cannot be moved.'

'What responsibilities?'

'Private responsibilities.'

'Trust when I say, traveler, you do not want both the merchant guild and the church as adversaries.'

Plates of tarts, puddings, custards, wafers, patties, doughnuts, pancakes, and many more sugary cakes were delivered in succession by a parade of stiff and unsmiling congregants. The priest helped himself to multiples of each.

'The church does not require weaponry to wage war,' the priest said while he sucked sugar from each of his fingers.

'Service begins at sundown then?'

The priest grinned and stood and said to the congregants attending him, 'I'll take my afternoon bath.' They escorted him from the hall.

'Pardon? May I have this to go?' the traveler said of the heaps of food in front of him.

Congregants removed it and left him alone in the dining hall. The boy was pushed in and the door shut behind him.

'No food and no light was brought,' the boy said.

When it was clear the traveler and the boy had been abandoned, they quietly departed. Upon their return, the traveler was quick to have the boy clear out the guard post's undercroft, which was filled with wooden weapon racks, tarp-covered furniture, barrels of spoiled beer and wine, chests, stained linens, carpets eaten by mildew and mold, human feces, animal feces, pest animal bones, pest animals in other states of decay, burlap sacks filled with rotted vegetables, adult and children's clothing perforated by animal teeth, and hundreds of dead insects.

The boy wove through the undercroft then said, 'Nobody thought to donate these goods while still fresh or intact?'

'And risk lawsuit for illness or injury of said goods, even in an unsoured state? And we must not forget about logistics. Who would then store these goods? How would they get there, and which agency would facilitate disbursement?'

'You can't just give it?'

'Safer to let it rot.'

The boy became quiet and stone-faced for a long moment, and he changed the subject.

'Why must this undercroft be cleared and in such haste?'

'To make room, of course.'

'Room for what?'

'Your unending curiosity annoys me,' the traveler said. The boy attempted to respond but the traveler left him to begin work.

While the boy worked, the traveler instructed the volunteer guard on many lessons in the courtyard and through the afternoon.

They stood with dirty faces and listened and held improvised weapons of pitchforks, scythes, cleavers, rope, swages, hammers, wooden boards with broken nail, whips, saws, axes both sharp and dull, gimlets, mallets that were rusted, spades, and shears they had brought from their homes.

The lesson concluded and the traveler called for questions. One timid villager who wielded a leather and sturdy boot raised his hand. 'I have a question.'

'Excellent. You question which part?' the traveler said.

'All of it.'

'All of it?'

'Yes, that's right.'

'You understood none of what I've said?'

'No need to be rude about it,' the villager said with a coarse scowl.

'Apologies.'

More villagers confessed the same. Calls to restart the lesson widened and escalated into a mean and uncoordinated cheer from the crowd and they raised their improvised weapons like a riled war band.

The traveler started the lesson from the beginning and delivered it with more care. He finished without interruption.

Carpenters were identified among the volunteer guardsmen and the traveler presented them drawings of defensive weapons to be built along the wall.

'These drawings are crude,' they told the traveler.

'You mistake crudeness with intention. These are designed with expertise. '

'These are queer and irrational,' they said. 'These are dangerous. Adjustments must be made.'

'There will be no adjustments. Years have been spent fine-tuning these specifications. Many brilliant and successful engineers of wood and of metal have consulted on each mechanism and approved without question. These will properly slay the giant. You must trust me.' Wood and other materials were sourced and procured, and construction began.

The traveler and the boy supervised and ensured the defenses were built exactly to plan.

CHAPTER SIX

A t sundown the volunteer guard assembled at the foot of the church's many steps for the evening's sermons.

They had worked through the day constructing the wall defenses and had finished and the traveler had ordered them to church.

Word spread of the volunteer guard's expected attendance through the village and villagers crowded the basin and baths to wash their face and their feet and remove the dirt and fecal matter from beneath their nails and argue with one another who was next. When the church doors opened, and then an hour later shut, all pews were densely packed with not one seat to spare. Excess villagers stood in the wings and in the rear and on the balconies and they held their children and the hands of their men and women.

Dusk's flame warmed the windows and spilled over the old stone and warned the church hall of the coming dark. Candles were tall and lit and drifts of sweet-scented smoke wandered silently through the pews. The cries of a baby and then an embarrassed mother bounced and then broke and the white noise of chatter and coughing and nose-picking stopped. Seated villagers adjusted and the pews groaned and then the hall was quiet and still, not a sound or breath. The organist was first to bring the service to motion and played, and the choir began their plainsong and harmony. Those seated stood and a prayer was led across the church, and they sat once more.

Congregants escorted the priest to the pulpit.

He wore vestments woven from fine fabrics and a bishop's headdress, though he was not a bishop. The priest beheld the filled pews and the filled wings and the filled balconies. He met eyes with the traveler, who sat in the front with the boy. The priest cleared his throat and fabricated a smile. He began.

'Serve the Lord and you will do strange things. Yes. You will not beat your wife and you will not drink to inebriation and return home and slap your children and throw them about your home. Become a servant of Him and you will do strange things. Holy is he who understands the notions of conduct and of dress, and of obligation. Therefore, as noblemen of the Lord, we are then just to consider commoners and peasants and diseased as animals, as daemons.'

Commoners and peasants in attendance nodded and agreed, and they smiled and looked down on each other but never themselves. They said, 'Amen!'

'Heretics speak of higher literacy. They wish to seduce the simple man with written word. They wish to be your master. Edification is a curse, lest ye be as Adam. And, too, the worst trap of men provided by the true enemy of the Lord, and the most difficult to evade; that of the woman. Beware the woman who does not submit.' Women across the church lifted their gaze to heaven and shut their eyes and nodded their heads and raised one palm to the Lord while the other went over their hearts.

They said, 'Amen!'

The priest opened a book that was not the Good Book but was masked as one.

He said, 'A frugal man who gave not to his church died and he did wake in perdition. He lifted his eyes and said, "Father Abraham, send Lazarus to dip the tip of his finger in water and touch my tongue, for I am in torment of these flames." Hell is a place of eternal fire. It burns your skin like the roasting pig and boils your organs and eyes and blood and cooks your meat and bones and scalds your crown and singes your hair and bakes your tongue.' The priest moved alongside the pulpit. He looked across the church to confirm all eyes were on him. They were, save for the traveler. He was sound asleep.

'I met a man in the fields. From nose to toe, his skin had burned and melted and scarred over. He was ugly and deformed. He shook my hand, and there was a secretion that came from his hand that nauseated me. He spoke not clearly, but I understood him with the Lord's aid, and he said, "I disobeyed the Lord and I did not give money unto my church and I did not heed my priest and I did not attend services regularly. I did work on an angry hearth and oil did spill on my skin and it did burn me to disability and, dear Lord, if that is what awaits me in hell then I never want to go to that place," and he pledged to obey the Lord and give money unto his church and to heed his priest so that he may never burn again. It was the greatest gift he'd been given. His body burned so that his soul could be saved.'

The priest allowed that to settle over the congregation. A smile appeared on the priest then waned then appeared and then waned again.

He said, 'The collection plates will now circulate.'

Assigned congregants moved from pew to pew and through the wings and through the balconies and collected coin from each and every villager. The choir sang plainsong. Several times the congregants needed to stop and swap full plates for empty ones. The boy had no money and received a sullen look from the congregants and the priest, and they made record of his failure. A handful of others were also recorded for their monetary inability.

When the plate came to the traveler, he excused himself to the latrine and returned when collection had ceased.

Communion of stale bread and old wine was given. The traveler went for a second serving. The priest continued the sermon well into the night. He concluded by saying, 'The Lord has spoken to me. He told unto me that no giant comes and we are not to listen to such claims. The Lord will forever keep us and defend us. He loves our village above all others. My flock, we have no need for a volunteer guard. What we do have need for is you here, in His home, giving to your church.' The priest looked down on the traveler and smiled and scratched an itch below his waist while the congregation cried Amen. The priest's hand returned from below discolored and soiled. He rubbed his hand on his robe.

The boy said, 'He must understand how unseemly that appears.'

'The congregation doesn't seem to mind.'

The starved man stood and shouted in defense of the volunteer guard and the traveler for all the church to hear and the congregation replied with boos.

The starved man moved through aisles and said, 'They fed me and housed me when none here would!'

Congregants quickly removed him.

The woman pulled and fought to free him, but she, too, was removed. Other members of the volunteer guard joined and were also removed.

'Collection plates will now make rounds once more,' the priest said.

In lieu of collection plates, which had all been filled, congregants stepped through pews and wings and balconies and required villagers dump their coin into cloth sacks.

It was after midnight when the service ended. Villagers returned to their homes tired and poor.

The traveler remained seated when all had gone.

'You look worried,' the boy said.

The traveler said, 'I do not worry.'

'But you look it.'

The boy meditated before bed for peace and focus and awareness. The boy taught this to the traveler and he heard him, late in the night, practice a speech in his quarters but could not make out the words. Together they rose with the sun and meditated with the morning. Summer warmth spread over the land.

Volunteer guardsmen arrived and the traveler assigned patrol routes through the village. An eye, he said, was to be kept for any sign of their coming foe. Some were to patrol the streets, others were to patrol the village walls. The boy handed each patrol group a whistle from the traveler's belongings.

'Patrol is wretched on my feet,' a villager said.

'Can a patrol exemption be obtained?' another said.

'Has patrol been proven effective?' yet another said and, if proven, several villagers demanded they be provided evidence.

'My cousin says patrol causes disease,' a villager from the back shouted. Others shouted they had heard the same.

'All concerns will be examined,' the traveler said.

'They will?' the boy said.

'No,' the traveler said in an aside. The volunteer guardsmen parted and began their patrols. For many days and nights the volunteer guardsmen trained and patrolled, and they enjoyed many donations of food and drink and many days free from labor obligations. No giant came. Doubt quickly bloomed. First there were discussions, then there were questions. Still no giant came. Village scholars made declarations of their opinion as studied men and in open courtyards told villagers who came to listen that there is almost certainly no giant and even if there were it would be harmless and would simply pass on.

Parchment was hung about the village. Each read the same: Skawlers Say No Jeyent Cums.

One morning, the traveler pulled the boy from bed and into motion.

'We have need to see the elder.'

They walked the village while morning broke and the people stirred. Villagers went about with crosses held tight.

The traveler bid a passing mother good morning. A look of disgust wrinkled her face, and she hurried onward.

A villager wearing a bright band around his arm in support of the volunteer guard crossed the morning path of a farmer pulling his harvest into market. The traveler and the boy witnessed several heated words exchanged.

The farmer shoved the villager and shouted and shoved him again.

'When you wear that pin, you further the agenda that condemns this village! No giant comes! The Lord says so!' The villager sought to walk away, but the farmer jerked the man by the hair and pulled him to the cobblestone and kept him there. 'Sheep!' he screamed into the villager's face. Spit ejected onto the villager's cheeks and forehead. The farmer prevented the villager from standing. 'Sheep!' Others joined in shouting into the villager's face. 'Sheep!'

The traveler and the boy detoured onto a different street. They heard the shouting continue.

Upon arrival, the traveler and the boy were taken to the village hall's inner chamber, where the public were not allowed. Inside, the elder lounged with a crowd of noblemen and noblewomen who matched his young age. Set between them was a tall hookah packed with Tumbak tobacco.

Long blankets of smoke hung in the air and the elder and his noblemen and noblewomen took turns smoking and exhaling with terrible coughs, choking the air further.

'Apologies for the interruption,' the traveler said.

'He does not look knowledgeable of giants,' the noblemen and noblewomen said.

'Pardon?'

The nobles smoked and coughed and passed the hookah to the boy and they grew frustrated when he refused.

'You do not smoke?'

'I cannot.'

They shoved the hookah at the boy.

'Polished men smoke.'

'Wonderful for polished men,' the boy said.

'By chance, has news of the watchmen who rode on the giant returned?' the traveler asked of the elder.

'I expected the messenger this morning. He is late,' the elder said.

'Excellent.'

'You fear the smoke?'

'No,' the boy said. There was a crack in his voice.

'The boy fears smoke!' the nobles said and they laughed and smoked and coughed.

'My breath is shallow. Smoke from a great fire damaged my lungs,' the boy said, but the noblemen and noblewomen laughed and did not hear him.

'It displeases me to say I bring word of significant developments,' the traveler said nearer the elder.

'Significant developments?' The elder took the hookah hose and drew a deep inhale. He released a cloud of smoke from his nostrils and lay onto a pillow quite relaxed.

'I am compelled to action,' the traveler said.

'Men knowledgeable of giants do not look like him,' the noblemen and noblewomen said aloud.

'What do they look like?' the boy said.

'Not him.'

'It is no secret giants are bedeviled by wealth,' the traveler said.

'We are a wealthy village,' the elder said.

'When the giant attacks, it will first seek jewels and coin and valuables.'

The elder looked upon his jewels and coin and valuables strewn about the inner chamber. 'That's a problem,' the elder said.

'You must collect all the village's wealth,' the traveler said.

'I must?'

'Allow me to defend it from the giant.'

The boy twisted and scrutinized the traveler. In return, the traveler avoided the boy's gaze, which lasted for several uncomfortable moments.

'What thoughts have you?' the elder asked of the noblemen and noblewomen. They were smoking and coughing and had not been listening.

'He does not look knowledgeable of giants,' they said. They spoke for the elder further. 'Why has the giant not come? Where is the creature?'

'En route, surely to arrive any day.'

'Perhaps it comes not at all,' the elder said.

'My own eyes have seen the giant. It stands tall as any mountain. One eye does not match in size; it is bulged and enlarged and yellow as morning piss. The head is bald and blistered over, and from its mouth comes drool of a foul color. It is obese with the spoils of its appetite and fury and its looting. A smell follows it, a putrid, gagging odor. It is the rotten man meat accumulated in its teeth and which lingers on its tongue, and it is nude as the day the earth birthed the thing unto us.'

The nobles coughed and said, 'This man has never seen a giant.'

'I am bored of giant talk,' the elder said. 'Enough has been invested in you, traveler. I tire of the noise from the church and the merchants. I decree the volunteer guard disband and depart one another. Let's return the people to work. Please leave the village at your convenience.'

He lay back down and smoked and coughed with the noblemen and noblewomen.

The traveler and the boy were deposited outside and the door was swiftly shut behind them.

'You did not mention the village's wealth before?'

The traveler kept a quicker pace than the boy.

'Do not avoid the question,' the boy said to the traveler's back.

'Do not follow me.'

'What have I done?'

'You bombard with endless questions and find no satisfaction in the answers. You waste my time in this back and forth. You distrust all my resolutions. You seek surprise and are surprised when you find it. You locate your nose amidst matters in which it has no permission. I have no use for you.'

'Then why help this orphan on that empty road?'

'Trust when I say I wish I had not.'

The boy followed the traveler.

The traveler faced the boy and released a scream. 'Stop following me!'

The boy recoiled.

The traveler marched down the cobblestone and defended his sharp focus from merchants who openly protested and demanded their workers return before the village hall and from villagers who greeted him without invitation and scolded him and offered him opinions unrequested.

Some followed. Others watched.

The traveler ran and evaded and disappeared from the boy and from sight.

CHAPTER SEVEN

The boy sat atop the village wall. Beside him were the starved man and the woman who he had joined several hours earlier. He had come to them upset and they had asked no questions but had received him and had kept him company. They had not spoken a word between them.

A clear night swirled above and the valley spread below the wall and before them and became wide and sharp. Starlight punctured the trees and washed the grassland and it mirrored in the ponds. The roads forked and twisted and divided the valley and were, but for the rabbits and skunks and mice and wolves, empty at this hour.

'We shall be the first to see the giant. I do not care the guard is disbanded,' the woman said.

'I do care,' the starved man said.

'We shall be first and hailed as heroes.'

'I do not care to be first. I do not care to slay the giant.'

'If we are heroes, we can do and go as we please. I will slay the giant and leave and not return.'

'I wish you would not. I wish you would not leave.'

'The guard is disbanded. I do not care.'

'Donations of food frequented my table as thanks. The guard is disbanded, now they will end.'

'You cannot feed yourself?' the boy said. It was the first he had spoken. The starved man kept many shadows from the starlight and remained silent as a mountain.

'I will leave. I will leave alone. I will leave all behind when the giant lay still,' the woman said.

'It is no kinder beyond these walls than within them.'

'He is right,' the boy said. 'The world's madness spares no place.'

'I will leave alone.'

They ate a snack of bread and cheese and spoke no more. They continued patrol down the southern wall. Two villagers met them on the eastern wall and barred the way forward. One had an uncombed beard and dark-brown eyes and long arms. The other was large in the waist and broad-shouldered and wore ill-fitted clothing.

The boy knew them to be failed applicants for the volunteer guard.

'Away with you,' the woman said.

The wide one spoke first. 'We will not move.'

'We will not move for sheep,' the long-armed one said.

'It is conspiracy,' the wide one said. 'They wish you to believe a giant comes. They wish to control you!'

'You will not control us,' the long-armed one said.

The wide one intruded the boy's personal space to an uncomfortable degree and came short of pushing him. He wagged his finger and pointed in all manner of direction. 'The Lord saves from all foes seen and unseen!' he said. He repeated it an obscene number of times. The starved man, the woman, and the boy aimed to walk around the boasters, who had gone red in the face and formed fists and cried out for revolution, for uprising, and cried out that they were victims and that a slippery slope had begun and that their children had no future in such despotism. Watchmen had heard them and came and took them away, and they kicked and wrestled and claimed unjust treatment until distance quieted them.

Some hours later, the starved man, the woman, and the boy passed the village tavern. An invitation was offered for dinner and ale at no charge for their bravery and sacrifice in service of the volunteer guard. Remorse, too, was given for news of the guard's dissolution. The starved man and the woman and the boy happily received the meal of roasted chicken, bread, porridge, gravy, raisins, ham, cheese, goose, and fruits that were in season and fresh. The starved man and the woman drank wine, beer, and heavy ale to excess.

The food preparer emerged and gave personal thanks. He said that many years prior, he believed he had seen a giant and believed it meant to harm him, and shortly after his wife succumbed to a weakened heart. He said he connected the two events and now harbored great hatred for giants and hoped the giant would come so that it may be slain. He would dance on its corpse and spit in its dead mouth. A matter required he return to the kitchen, and he dismissed himself.

Late into the meal, the woman refused food and only accepted drink. Food continued to the starved man. The boy watched with distaste and touched his meal very little. He had not noticed before the starved man's weight gain. His cheeks and belly had rounded. Service stopped, and yet the starved man and woman demanded more and were then asked to leave. The boy escorted them. The starved man and the woman walked without balance and were red in the cheeks, and their words came at great difficulty and slow in pace. They walked empty streets lit by oil lanterns. Homes were dark. They were alone.

'I did not fall on hard times. Times have always been hard,' the starved man said. He stood on the edge of tears. The boy helped him balance his steps forward.

They entered a darker range of the village where there were no lanterns, and the way forward was lit only by star and moonlight. Shadows were long and misleading. The wide man and the long-armed man sprang from darkened corners and once again barred the way forward for the starved man, the woman, and the boy.

'The volunteer guard was disbanded. Cease all involvement!' they demanded.

They jittered with anger and the veins in their necks bulged. They seemed quite volatile.

'We refuse,' the woman said. Drink had made her loose, but before the two men she grew firm and her face held no sign of pity.

The wide one berated the woman with a barking nonsense and was cut short by the woman's fist. In response, the long-armed one advanced on her and also met her fist. Drunken screams broke from the woman and she kicked and kneed and brought her fists down upon the prone men and unleashed a deep anger across their crumpled forms and did not cease or lose momentum. She carried on, even after the boy had helped the starved man away and they were out of sight.

The boy delivered the starved man to his home, which was no home but a shed of tools in the middle of an empty lot of bare earth. The lack of door gave view to a bed of straw and soiled clothing in a pile.

'My children are dead in the ground. I could not feed them,' the starved man said. He cowered into the shed and lay in the straw bed.

The boy lingered. The starved man said, 'Please leave,' and the boy returned to the guard post. The traveler was not there, though his things were still littered about his quarters. The boy slept and in the morning woke to those loyal to the volunteer guard amassed outside the guard post in the cold morning air. The woman had gathered them and now stood at their head. Her eyes were red from lack of sleep and her hair was greasy from lack of wash.

'We persevere,' she said. 'No decree can halt our love for this village and our devotion to defend it. We shall lay down our lives in service if the traveler should need.'

The amassed crowd chanted the same.

'We lay down our lives if the traveler needs!'

'He is not here,' the boy said. 'And we must consider that perhaps no giant comes.'

'Oh,' the woman said.

The chants ceased, and the crowd looked amongst itself for guidance, and a garrison of watchmen with clubs and swords drawn marched on the crowd and beat the jobless to the dirt and into submission and carried them away and returned them to their places of employment. The boy hurried into the guard post and watched from the window. The crowd broke in two and reformed their ranks, and an effort was made to resist through a brutal charge on the watchmen led by farmers and barkeeps and millers and carpenters and smithies who raised their fists up high and who shouted with vigor, but they were met with clubs and were pounded and punched and kicked and yanked and were swiftly quelled. The woman withstood the watchmen and fought and bloodied several of their number but was overwhelmed and pinned and kicked until the fight left her. When the unrest was subdued, the ground was littered with volunteer guardsmen. They moaned and rolled and wept and crawled and bled in the dirt, like beaten dogs, like scolded and beaten and ashamed dogs forced into the corner, and about them and through them the watchmen moved, and the boy watched them drag away the beaten until only the woman was left. One watchman pulled her through the dirt by the hair, and she threatened and then pleaded for excusal.

'Back to the bakery with you,' the watchmen said.

'A dark prison cell would be a blessing opposite that awful place. Complaints have been filed against my employer, the baker!' she said. Tears bore down her dirtied cheeks. She said to those watching, 'He does assault me in perverse ways and no action has been taken. No punishment has been brought upon him! He will bring it upon me!'

They dragged her away and informed passing and concerned villagers to ignore her screaming lies.

The boy gathered what few belongings he had and drafted a note for the traveler, should he return.

"It is to the road I return. Perhaps the road shall lead me, or perhaps it is only ever the road which I am to know and find solitary comfort within.

- The Boy."

He left the note on the traveler's pillow and took a final look around the guard post, then departed. He crossed the village. The great doors of the wall opened, and a caravan of a dozen men and women and several small children hurried inside and blocked the boy's departure.

The men of the caravan pulled wagons filled with belongings and injured. Filth covered their faces and robes, and fear colored their eyes. Several appeared haphazardly cared for and wailed in pain.

Others stared absently with bloodshot eyes. They shivered though it was not cold. Some openly wept.

An elderly man parted from the scared and pained and traumatized.

The boy said, 'From what horrors do you run?'

'We run from the giant,' the elderly man said.

CHAPTER EIGHT

O il lanterns burned within the church late into the night. Villagers left their beds and homes and gathered beneath the church's steeple to glimpse on the displaced peoples who had been ushered inside to be administered care.

Pews had been rearranged and made comfortable with blankets and wool. Refugees, as they had been called, lay along the pews and in the wings and atop the balconies.

Congregants carried those that could not walk and helped those who had no strength to drink water and eat food from the church's bountiful stores. Bandages and supplies were hurried to where they were needed and the priest gave a sermon of comfort from the pulpit and it did comfort and calm those who listened. The boy wrapped the arm of the elderly man in bandage and chanced glances at his empty face and kept him company with silence against the groans and lament that crowded the church hall. Foot traffic fussed between the aisles. The boy finished with the elderly man's bandage and sat with him for an hour.

Congregants divided as priority required, most continued hurried medical care, others documented testimony of events as dictated to them.

The traveler found the boy but gave priority to the elderly man.

'You saw the giant?'

'With my own eyes.'

'Oh, dear.'

A thought occupied the traveler. He felt for a place to sit as though he mistrusted his own vision.

'It tore my cattle in two and pressed my wife until she burst like rotted fruit.' The elderly man wailed and cursed his own cowardice and stood and shook his fists at the Lord and wailed louder so that the whole of the church turned their attention to him, which only fueled his production. Spit exploded from his lips. His hair was mottled with sweat. The church's ceiling resounded his bitter insults, and then he twisted to face the villagers who had come in from the night, driven by curiosity, and he recounted to them the abhorrence that had befallen his and his fellow refugees' home.

When he was finished, the villagers stood with mouths open and eyes wide, and a few fled for their homes. The elderly man's graphic depiction caused a wife to faint into her husband's arms. The elderly man sank into fits of anguish on his knees and when the whole of the church had returned their attention to their own matters and when the villagers had made themselves gone, he sat once more. The boy held the elderly man's quaking hand and offered his sympathy.

Congregants brought food. The elderly man ate, he was ravenous and the boy had issue watching it.

While refugees were served and also ate in quiet, congregants consoled and drew many warm baths and washed the refugees and wrapped them in clean church linen.

The traveler and the boy remained in the furthest pew well after the refugees had lost their battle with fatigue and had gone to sleep on coverlets and plain pillows strewn about the nave, and there the traveler and the boy sat until morning met the church doors and punctured the stuffy hall.

Memorial flowers had been laid at the church's feet and were tranquil and vivid in dawn's wakeful light. Small white crosses had been planted in the dirt and grass, and wreaths had been hung on their necks. Villagers kneeled at the crosses and begged the Lord to protect their families and to ensure the prosperity of their ventures and to allay their illnesses and to keep their love faithful despite temptations and to maintain the foundations of their homes and to fill their fields with a most bountiful and healthy crop. Only then was a brief and bored prayer offered for the refugees, amen, and the crosses were abandoned. One toppled, and no one bothered to right it.

The traveler and the boy sat on the church steps and allowed the sun to warm away the sorrow which heavied their shoulders and tensed their temples, for a solid and peculiar quiet lay about the village streets where the movement of bodies and work animals and commerce, at this hour, should have been present but were not.

The traveler handed the boy's note to the boy and said, 'Do you still wish to leave?'

'Before the refugees' arrival, I held doubt in your claim. I was wrong to withhold trust. I am sorry.'

The traveler opened his bag.

'For my behavior toward you, I too am sorry,' he said. He presented a meditation throw made of dark-blue fleece. 'The stone and straw shall plague your knees no longer.'

The boy examined the throw and rubbed the fleece between his fingers and on his face.

'My father had a throw such as this. My mother made it. He meditated on it often.'

'He sounds progressive indeed.'

'He shared his learnings from the east. Villagers turned from the church's piety and sermons of fear and its hoard of wealth. Together he and the villagers meditated before many sunrises. There was peace in the street where once there had been anger and exclusion and hate and entitlement. It was not long until the church caught rumor. I was asked by the clergy to confess my father's heresy. They told me be not afraid; my admission would save my father and my family. They told me the Lord would value my courage and welcome me to His bosom. They told me when I die, my flesh would rise again and enter into eternity. So. I confessed. Clergymen entered our home mid night and removed my father and mother and sister from their beds. They held them for three days. They were not fed nor were given water. On the fourth day, their hands and feet were bound to stakes and fixed upright to face the dusk. Then pouches of gunpowder were tied to their throats. They did this while my mother and sister wept and pleaded for freedom. My father was not a stoic man, but before them he remained as such. A priest accused them of their betrayal to the Lord God and made known to them my confession and read a prayer from the Good Book. The choir sang hymns, and the clergy lit a pyre and celebrated the cooking of their flesh and the volume of their screams. The gunpowder around their necks detonated—and their screams were stopped, but the fire continued until dawn. The church abandoned them there. I took them down and laid them in the earth. I then set about the road. That was some time ago.'

The traveler could find no words and so embraced the boy, and a moment later, the boy reciprocated. The traveler said, 'We are not meant to extend our loneliness intentionally.' The traveler held him tight. 'Will you be at my side when the giant comes?'

'I would be no place else,' the boy said.

A messenger interrupted to announce they were summoned by the elder and took them at once to the inner chamber of the village hall. The elder was seated with his noblemen and noblewomen, the priest, and the head of the merchant guild. The elder's wealth and jewelry that had cluttered the chamber's corners were now arranged into a dozen cloth sacks the size of small children. The seated faced the traveler and the boy and met them with large welcoming smiles and eyes full of relief.

'Thank the Lord,' the elder said.

The noblemen and noblewomen stood and helped the traveler to a seat. The boy was left by the door. To the traveler's surprise, wine was brought for him and his feet were placed on an ottoman. Fat, ripe grapes were force fed to him.

'A masseuse awaits, should you prefer one.'

The traveler searched over each shoulder. Again he was met with smiles from the priest, the noblemen and women, and the head of the merchant guild.

'I do prefer, perhaps later.'

'We were just in receipt of the priest's account of the refugees,' the elder said.

'Thank the Lord, not one among their number was of severe injury, nor fatal cut, nor broken bone, nor illness, nor fever. The hand of the Lord truly intervened and shepherded those fearful flock unto us. Requested subsidies for their care were much appreciated and welcomed, dear elder,' the priest said.

The elder said, 'The dismissal of your warning of the giant and of your concern for the village's wealth was regretful and, might I say, not at all my fault,' the elder said. 'My noblemen and noblewomen are to blame for my lapse in judgment, and they submit, in writing, a request of forgiveness.'

The noblemen and women grumbled and were silenced. The elder forced them to offer their formal request which the traveler accepted.

'Surely a leader can't be expected to make every decision a sound one,' the traveler said.

'A thought I repeat in this chamber often.'

'No doubt.'

The priest and the head of the merchant guild shared looks of impatience with the elder.

'We have a request.'

The traveler then noticed the congregants and merchants dressed in high-priced robes who stood with smiles in the shadows across the chamber and who looked at him and nowhere else. They held bags of coin and jewels and pointed west, one and all.

'Make your request. I am listening.'

'Our request is this: protect our wealth from the giant.'

'I could not possibly.'

The priest stood and read from the Good Book. '"I am come that they might have life, and that they might have it more abundantly."' He shut the book and said, 'The message is clear. The Lord wishes our wealth preserved. A church without funds crumbles to the evil of the Morningstar, and without its beacon of goodness and equality, man is reduced to savagery. How else might His work be done? How else might His Word reach the heathens of the East? How else would this village and its sinners find redemption? How else would its sins be washed away like the dirt of the Lord's supple feet? How else would the moral compass of man endure? How else would women know their place beneath men? To whom then go the impoverished and tithe? The Lord blesses our wealth. It is spoken to me from the lips of angels.'

'Spoken while you sleep in your silken bed?' the boy said.

'The Lord wishes I sleep in a silken bed.' The priest sat and did not speak or look at the traveler again.

The head of the merchant guild brought his fist down and said, 'A village relies on production and acquisition and exchange and capital! How else does a market offer unneeded goods and services? How else does a businessman haggle with the diligent and famished farmer for low-cost corn and grain? How else would the young and the elderly be compelled to spend all their earned coin? A village that cannot answer these descends into ruination.'

'Our request has been stated. What say you?' the elder said.

'The volunteer guard and my substantial wage will be reinstated?'

The head of the merchant guild lent the elder an intimidating eye.

'You may have those without labor obligations.'

'No good.'

'And a more substantial wage,' the elder said.

'Fine,' the traveler said. He poured another glass of wine and drank and delighted in the taste and said, 'I suppose I could defend such a sum if it were amassed in, say, one location.'

'Anywhere of your choosing,' the elder said.

'Yes, anywhere,' the others said.

'The guard post's undercroft could prove suitable for such a defense.'

'It will be done.'

The traveler quickly added, 'The apothecary, too, has a valuable herb that must be protected from the giant.'

'Yes, yes, anything you say,' the elder said.

Noblemen and noblewomen and congregants and merchants loaded the mass of their wealth and that of their leaders onto a wooden cart.

The traveler watched and drank wine, and the boy made faces at the congregants. A pile of wealth some ten feet high weighed down the wagon, and it required a force of men and horses to cart it through the village.

The traveler and the boy followed.

Villagers in the streets came and marveled at such an accumulation of riches, assets, and deeds. They ran into their homes to gather family so they too might witness the hoarded reserves marched forth from the village hall.

A grand following of beggared villagers formed and cheered for the wealth and defended any accusations against the wealth and assembled into barriers and bullied one another and begged to gift their coin and valuables to the wealthy and cried out in thanks to the wealthy for their compassion and their generosity and all the opportunities they had created.

'Why do the needy love the rich so?' the boy said.

'Not a civilization on this earth has flourished into overabundance without collusive speech to a slow mind.'

The beggared following stood watch over the nobles and congregants and merchants and audited their movements while the cart was unloaded into the guard post's undercroft. A homeless man was seen to pocket a single coin and was pulled into the starving crowd and scolded and beaten and stripped and made to leave the village for good.

The cart was empty of wealth as the day ended. A lock was placed on the undercroft, and the traveler retained the key.

'I grant the assurance that no harm will fall upon the wealth housed within,' the traveler announced to the beggared following, the noblemen and noblewomen, the congregants, and the merchants. They thanked him and departed, and the night was quiet.

The boy made coffee and together he and the traveler drank its bitter warmth and reheated a donated stew over fire beneath the stars.

A congregant approached the traveler and said, 'The priest would have you speak to the refugees. Calm is needed for them. The giant yet enters their nightmares.'

'Must I?'

'I was instructed upon refusal to recite to you the evening sermon.'

'I shall arrive in the morning.'

The boy and the traveler ate stew and watched the stars and then retired to sleep. A noise woke the boy late in the night, one that was not unlike the opening of the undercroft door. He heard no more sound, and sleep lay upon him once again.

CHAPTER NINE

As promised, the traveler and the boy rose before the sun. The boy prepared breakfast. Insect chirps annoyed his want for quiet. Both he and the traveler ate with tired scowls.

On the way to the church, the traveler and the boy passed the bakery. It was yet early and the doors were not open, but smoke climbed from its chimney and candlelight blossomed within its frosted windows. The woman filled a display with fresh breads and pastries and tarts and cakes. A bruise had swollen over her eye and another over her lip. Her hands trembled and her clothes were loose and stretched and roughed about. Her eyes were red and wet, but her cheeks were dry. She paused several times to collect herself. She met eyes with the traveler and the boy but was called into the back by an angered voice. She froze in place.

The voice called again and startled her with its violence, and she disappeared into the back. She did not reemerge.

The traveler and the boy reached the church, where a morning sermon had just begun. They stood in the wings as outside observers and the refugees were made to stand before the congregation and recount the evils that had befallen them and their loved ones and their homes. Many eyes in the audience turned away with aversion, and many congregants dismissed themselves with stomachs twisted into knots.

The refugees were then encouraged, forcefully, to give thanks to the Lord, and the priest explained to them that their village was good and happy and almost certainly dependent upon the material, and the Lord reminded them, through the giant, He must be the source of their happiness and that without His grace their survival was not ensured. Collection plates were passed, and the congregation was eager to fill them to overflow.The congregants praised Him, amen.

One refugee questioned the priest and said, 'The Lord said, "My children are too happy and fulfilled, I must deliver them ruin"?'

'His ways are mysterious to us,' the priest said.

'Could the Lord not have given reminder without the deaths of our friends and family and without allowing the giant to level our village so cruelly?'

'A goodness we cannot see will come of this, His word tells us. Give thanks.'

'You ask I celebrate loss and tragedy for unknown benefit?'

The priest motioned and congregants removed the refugee from the church. The congregants praised Him, amen, and tithed once more, and the sermon concluded. Pews and wings emptied, and the noise and chatter exited the church hall. The traveler and the boy joined on the frontmost pew the elderly man.

'I am told trauma from the giant remains among you,' the traveler said.

'What?'

'Your mortal spirit, it is in unrest.'

'Oh, yes. Terrible unrest,' the elderly man said. He studied the cross made of gold mounted behind the pulpit. 'If you guessed that cross's weight, what might you say?'

'I, too, have seen the giant.'

The elderly man turned from the cross and said, 'You have?'

'It destroyed my home as well and took from me my lover. I think often of her final look. It stays and will not leave.'

'I see.' The elderly man turned back to the cross. The pew groaned beneath him. Sunlight fell through the window and draped the cross in warm honey light. 'A quarter weight? Perhaps a hundredweight?'

'The loss of my home and my love emptied me. The same emptiness must harass you.'

'Is it bolted in place?'

'What?'

'The cross, is it bolted?'

The traveler and the boy shared a confused look.

'You look familiar,' the elderly man told the traveler.

'I do?'

'Has travel taken you to the westerly lands or to the northern isles?'

'No. Never.'

'Our paths have crossed; I feel certain of it.'

'I have a good memory for faces, elderly man, and yours I've undoubtedly not seen before.'

'Yes, I remember a village was very irate with you.'

'Was not me,' the traveler said toward the boy.

'Yes, I think it was.'

'Perhaps more than a hundredweight?' The traveler stood and moved toward the cross.

'It must be less than a hundredweight, I'd bet on it,' the elderly man said. He stood and further studied the cross alongside the traveler.

* * *

Midday, the traveler and the boy quit the church, which the traveler had rather hurriedly instigated. They were to meet the few volunteers without labor obligations they could muster, and once again passed the bakery, where a large number of workers had, once again, abandoned their responsibilities and gathered.

Some bore the broken bones and healing wounds of the clash with watchmen the day prior.

They shouted wrathful disagreements and targeted them upon the bakery. The content and volume of their offense drew more and more into their number.

The woman stood before them and encouraged their unrestraint. 'We revolt!'

'Revolt!' the workers repeated. 'Shame upon the merchants!'

'Shame!'

'Shame upon them for low wages!' a worker shouted.

'Shame!'

'Shame upon them for long hours!' another worker shouted.

'Shame!'

The woman turned to the bakery and shouted against its window, 'Shame upon them for the blame they place on you when you have done no wrong and the disguised words they exercise to lower our dignity. Shame on them for their lust for our time. Shame on them for their sugary criticisms and their pressure that compounds and squeezes and their distractions. Shame on them for the lies! Shame on them for our abuse and humiliation and pain!'

The crowd of workers had gone silent, and the woman cried before them. Sympathy and respect shone in their eyes, even when the woman lifted a stone and screamed and threw it through the bakery window. She turned to the crowd, and they continued their respect for her until the watchmen descended on them with clubs and beat their heads and necks and wrists and jaws. They called the workers filth and lazy and dangerous.

The workers fought back and injured many watchmen. A vigor filled the workers, and their cries drowned out the watchmen. Fear spread through the watchmen and they drew their swords and stayed the workers. The woman lifted a second stone and was run through by a novice watchman no more than a year into his manhood. The blade occupied the meat of her neck and chin and nose. She fell as stone. The watchman ran up the street in tears and with mighty sobs and screams. The woman lay on the cobblestone with her eyes and mouth open and her body rumpled and limp and her limbs at odd angles.

The crowd of workers were silent. The traveler and the boy were silent. The watchmen were silent. The workers screamed and were dispersed, save for the starved man who kept companionship with the woman's deserted body. After dinner, the body was collected, but the starved man lingered on the cobblestone and observed the woman's blood.

The woman's employer, the baker, washed the cobblestone when the sun had gone down and when flies had found the smell. None from the watchmen returned to explain the error or the senselessness, or to give apology or offer restitution. The night was empty of people and empty of sound, but for the traveler, the boy, and the starved man.

It was the starved man who receded into the night first. The boy meant to follow but the traveler placed a hand on his shoulder and held him still.

'I see no good reason to follow.'

'But he has no one.'

'He does not depart to grieve,' the traveler said. 'He departs with anger.'

'I am too familiar; that is why I should follow.'

'One cannot live as him and not be strong to events such as these. Time will calm him.'

'Or worsen him.'

'Leave him be now. Let us to bed. Tomorrow we patrol.'

They looked once more upon the lantern light that shone down on the woman's death place. The baker hung a wool blanket over the broken window and smothered the candle flames that burned within.

The baker did not give the woman's death place a second look as he departed.

CHAPTER TEN

The traveler and the boy were accompanied by the few volunteer guardsmen allowed to rejoin. They had patrolled the eastern wall that faced the wide plain and the blue lakes that led to the sea. The sun had risen from their waters and lit the waves aflame and burned the night from the sky. Patrol drew them from the eastern wall and along the southern face. A line of foreigners waited below for approved entry to the village, a line that extended well to the hills and further. The traveler and the boy and the volunteer guardsmen exchanged stories of the woman who had been struck down in the street. Not much was known of her.

One volunteer guardsman shared rumors of the woman's youth, that she had been a skilled painter and had gone to the west, to the large cities, to display her creations for the church and the nobility, and she had found fame but was exploited and made poor and then forced to return. Another volunteer guardsman shared rumor that none of that was true, that she had worked in her father's fields outside the village until she was a woman and had been married to a man who later died and had since taken any work made available to her. None present could confirm or deny that either story was true.

Neither the boy nor the traveler nor the volunteer guardsman offered a word to break the silence that followed, and so the volunteer guardsman said, 'How will we know when the giant draws close?'

'It will be unmistakable.'

'But how, exactly?'

'Well,' the traveler began. The boy, too, waited for his answer.

The traveler stood atop a wooden barrel and spoke down with animation. 'Silence always precedes the giant. Animals and insects hold sensitivity to the creature, as they do to a coming storm, and fear it and desert the land. One might witness their mass exodus to places of safety. Then follows the stench, before you've even laid eyes on the creature. It has been observed to cause even the most grizzled man to faint.'

'What then?'

The traveler hopped off the barrel and stomped along the village wall.

'What then? Then come the screams of those first to glimpse the awful creature and those first to receive its wrath. Then come the screams of those crushed beneath its bare feet and those mashed by its bare fist. Then come the screams of those buried within the homes it levels and those lifted off the ground and chewed within the creature's mouth.'

'What then?' said the boy.

The traveler ceased his animated gestures.

'What then? The giant delivers death and destruction until it tires or until there are no lives left to take or structures to shatter. Then it moves on.'

Darkened looks moved between the traveler, the boy, and the volunteer guardsman, and they could not help but turn to the valley and its empty vastness. It was peaceful, and the land was gentle and as of yet held no evidence of the giant's approach. A flock of white doves crossed into the valley and flew its length and disappeared.

The boy observed the traveler who was staring into the valley, and then the traveler said, 'I must check on the wealth.'

'I shall join,' the boy said.

'No need, finish patrol.'

'I am not needed here.'

'You are needed here.'

'He is not needed here,' the volunteer guardsman said.

The traveler looked at the volunteer guardsman for a long moment. He said, 'Very well, but it will be a boring and benign affair.'

'Boring and benign will be a welcome change of events,' the boy said. They made for the guard post and happened upon a memorial ceremony held in the shadow of the village hall. A platform had been erected in the early morning, and the elder and the head of the watchmen now stood atop. An image of the woman had been painted and was on display. Dark and sad colors had been used to give the woman form and depicted a sorrowful and pained appearance.

Disgruntled workers and dismissed volunteer guardsmen and everyday villagers had come to listen to the elder speak and waited before the platform for him to begin. Village watchmen held rank beneath the elder and kept watch over the memorial.

The traveler entered the crowd without warning, and the boy followed with some difficulty—the crowd was dense and their number large—but managed not to lose sight of him.

He matched the traveler's pace and pressed through gaps and shoulders and met him near the end of those gathered. The boy tugged on the traveler's coat, and when he saw the boy had reached him, he stopped where he stood. 'Do not pull my coat!'

'You broke into those gathered here so swiftly, I almost did not reach you.'

'Yes, well,' the traveler said, and his next words came with some challenge. 'I wanted a good view.'

The boy looked about. They were far from the platform, and those around them were much taller and obstructed most of the view.

'What of the wealth?'

'We must pay our respects,' the traveler said. He gave his attention to the elder, who was ready to begin but made many cursory turns in the guard post's direction.

'Let me begin with a comment that I am wholly shaken and horrified by the brutal death of—' The elder consulted his notes and flipped them. He did not find what he sought. 'Do any in attendance recall her name?'

None in the crowd did.

'I am wholly shaken and horrified by the brutal slaying of the woman. What can be said about her? Terrible incident, terrible, terrible, terrible incident. Those who bore witness could surely not conceive of any incident other than what was witnessed. Terrible, terrible, terrible. Horrible, horrible. I have the utmost dedication to the service of justice. She will not have perished in vain.'

The crowd applauded, and the elder basked in it.

The elder continued to read from his notes and did not lift his gaze to the crowd but kept it locked on the parchment. He said, 'But allowance cannot be given to crooked sayings of protest and instigation and acts of riot to mute the true victims in our midst, the merchants.' Boos erupted, but the elder did not pause. He read with indifference. 'In recent days, our village has suffered peril from nihilists and heretics and agitators who would level these blameless shops to ash, and let us not mention the loss in labor which keeps the good and decent people of this village in extended lines at the apothecary or the blacksmith or the market or the tailors or the jewelers.' The elder moved to the next parchment and continued to read with such dispassion. 'The loss in labor which keeps the farmer's wagon short of crops and fruits and vegetables and which increases the number of coin the good and decent people of this village must offer him.' Cheers hailed from the everyday villagers. 'I give the watchmen of this village full and martial authority over our streets. Law and order and civility will be forced as necessary.'

The head of the watchmen grinned and donned his battle helm and joined the ranks of his watchmen.

A cabbage struck the elder's nose, a second struck his temple, and a third made him cower. Watchmen enveloped the assemblage and dragged from it the disgruntled workers and dismissed volunteer guardsmen, to the cheers and applause of everyday villagers.

The starved man parted from the disorder with a small blade in hand and with a darkened look locked on the elder. He charged the platform and scaled its height. He pounced on the elder, who shrieked and wept and begged and received the blade into the soft of his shoulder. A column of watchmen towed the starved man free and stuck him with their swords in his belly and calf and throat and chest and hand, and even when he fell still, they continued. The elder was rushed to the village hall.

Panic spread, and the crowd stampeded in all manner of direction. The traveler escaped and made for the guard post without worry for the boy, who attempted to follow but was pushed and shoved and kicked and forced to the dirt. Bare feet and leather boots trampled him and he called out to the traveler for aid and cried out in pain. Conflict gave the traveler cause to stop, and he shifted focus between the street ahead and the boy and back again. He returned to the boy and wrenched him from the dirt, and they fled the turmoil and only slowed when they found an empty street.

The traveler sat the boy out of view and examined him for serious injury and found none beyond dark and terrible bruises and cuts and scrapes. The traveler tended these with cloth ripped from his sleeve.

'This village has lost all sense and reason,' the boy said.

'It had little to start with.'

'Is this every village? Is this how man behaves in all his lands?'

'You forget he is an animal. It is true he is smart, but his response and his emotion is animal.' The traveler stood the boy and said, 'Is your pain bearable?'

'I do not know anymore.'

'You're still expected to walk.'

The traveler led the boy to the guard post. Watchmen marched the cobblestone streets and pulled disgruntled laborers and dismissed volunteer guardsmen from hiding. The traveler and the boy found the guard post's door opened wide and the solid iron lock broken.

Inside they discovered the refugees with coin and jewels stuffed in their pockets, and they continued to stuff more and more and more with no awareness. Refugee mothers wrapped necklaces and large jewelry around their children's necks and wrists and shoved coin into their hands and their pockets.

'Pardon me,' the traveler said.

The refugees faced the traveler in unison. Some dropped the wealth they were holding; one ran out the door and up the street.

The contents of the elderly man's pockets weighed his trousers and they sagged on his waist. He kept them from falling to his ankles with one hand. A passing watchman entered and also saw the refugees mid-heist.

The elderly man released a sigh and then his pants, and they fell to his ankles.

He said, 'Could I speak with legal counsel?'

CHAPTER ELEVEN

The refugees were rounded up by the watchmen and assembled atop the platform before the village hall and placed on display for the villagers to come and observe. Their hands and feet were bound and they were each tied to posts and made to stand through the day and into the night. Signs were placed around their necks that read I STOLE YOUR WEALTH. Spit and insults and laughs fell on them and villagers pulled on the women's hair and punched the men and poured on them water and piss and other foulness, and none, not the small children or the frail elderly, were spared. A day in full sun had left them pink and blistered; some had managed sleep and needed waking. Others openly wept. Few maintained quiet and still anger.

While the village slept, the traveler and the boy brought leftover food donations and clean water. He instructed the boy to wash them of filth and ration the food so each could be fed.

The traveler woke the elderly man, who was in deep sleep. Drool ran down the folds of his chin and pooled on his shoulder.

'You have interrupted my dreaming,' the elderly man said.

'Terribly sorry.'

'What?'

'Pardon?'

'You have woken me. What do you want, traveler?'

'Have you hunger or thirst?'

The elderly man studied the boy, who helped a mother to water and then her son.

'You bring food and water to feed and wash us while all others bring ugliness?' the elderly man said.

The traveler gauged the boy's distance and leaned low and said, 'Earnest questions which plague me need answers.'

'Undo my bindings.'

'I cannot.'

'You will not.'

'I am respected in this village.'

'No, you're not. We heard the priest at night while the congregants waited on us hand and foot. He thinks you a fool.'

'He does?'

'They all do.'

'Why did you steal after receipt of such kindnesses?'

The elderly man gave his attention to the stars above and withheld his answer.

'Answer me.' The traveler raised his voice and drew the boy's attention without realization. He shouted, 'Did the giant truly level your village and displace you and your people? I must know.'

The question pulled the elderly man's curiosity, and a proud smile followed, but still no answer.

'No food or water for the rest,' the traveler said to the boy.

'But they are yet hungry and thirsty.'

The traveler took what food and water were left and threw them to the mud, then pulled the boy aside. 'I will not explain myself to you. Now come!'

Before the traveler and the boy departed, the elderly man said, 'I have remembered where I know you from.' He released a vigorous laugh, which shook his bound frame, and the laugh swelled and spread among the refugees, even the children, and their blended laughter ripped through the night, and it followed the traveler and the boy.

'In the morning, you will secure a wagon,' the traveler told the boy. A question was about to leave the boy's lips but, grounded in the traveler's coldness, he decided it was best he not give it voice.

Before dawn, the boy heard the traveler leave his bed and enter the undercroft and did not hear him come out again. The sun properly rose, and so did the boy. He knocked on the undercroft door with fresh breakfast and coffee in hand, but the traveler did not respond, and the door, with a new iron lock, remained sealed.

'You must eat,' the boy said through the door.

He ate his breakfast in the grass and left the traveler's on the table inside, even though it had gone cold, should he emerge. But he did not. As the traveler had asked, the boy sought a wagon and weaved through the streets, door to door. The boy came to a sizable home with many windows and doors and many servants who tended laundry in the yard and repaired worn finishes on the roof and washed the windows and scrubbed worn shoes. The boy asked for the head of the luxurious estate.

'What is your need for a wagon?' the noblewoman said.

'The need was not made known to me.'

'You follow uninformed requests made of you?' A baby cried from within the noblewoman's home. She turned from the door and demanded a servant tend the baby, which the boy could not see.

'The requester is trusted.'

'You know the requester well?'

'We have endured much. The weeks have bonded us.'

A pig laugh burst from the noblewoman and she cackled herself red in the face. 'What has convinced you the sum of a person can be understood in weeks so few?'

'I have confided in him.'

'My husband wedded me before I could seek my own path. He yielded three children to me and no more. His labors brought much prosperity upon this home. Many long days this family and this house were absent of him. Gifts and sugary compliments would often accompany his return. Fifteen summers our marriage made good. On a day like any other, I found two maids at my door. One told me my husband had fathered four of her children. The second told me her husband had run off with mine to live in apostasy. He has not since returned.' The baby cried again, and the noblewoman urged silence from both the servant and the baby.

The boy hid his unease with a nod and said, 'Have you a wagon?'

'Several.'

'Could one be borrowed for a day?'

'No,' the woman said. She shut the door, and the boy heard her shout at the servant and the baby for several minutes before he moved to the next home and then the next, and several more homes after. A couple, well into their gray seasons, listened to the boy's need for their old and beaten wagon and agreed, and the boy thanked them and pulled the rickety wagon across the village.

One wheel groaned and wobbled; the other was a size smaller and caused the wagon to lean left. Twice the boy nearly upended the wagon on the cobblestone, and then he did. It was too heavy for him to correct, so the boy flagged a hurried villager who ran and ate his lunch as he went.

'I cannot stop to help,' the hurried villager said. He took a bite of his lunch and chewed like a goat.

'But I cannot lift it.'

'I cannot miss the church's newest accusations!'

'Who is in receipt of these accusations?'

'Items were discovered in the refugees' belongings.'

'What items?'

'Damning items.'

The hurried villager joined a flow of curious villagers who also made for the platform where the refugees were still bound and where congregants stood and called the village to gather.

With none who desired to help, the boy wedged his fingers beneath the wagon and forced himself to lift its great weight. In the meat of the boy's back a sharp twist occurred and a pain like no other took him, but the wagon was righted and the task done. The boy, however, could not stand straight; it caused him outrageous agony and prevented him from full and deep breaths. Hunched over, he pulled the wagon to the edges of the congestion of villagers surrounding the platform. Rude villagers climbed into the boy's wagon and stood for a better view. He shooed them off, but they returned when the boy turned away.

'Dismount my wagon at once,' the boy said. The small chest movements required to speak caused him pain.

'We know this wagon,' the rude villagers said. 'It is not yours.'

'Off!'

Again, the rude villagers came off.

'Come! Come and hear!' the congregants called out. Church choir members filed onto the platform and formed a line behind the bound refugees. They began to sing, and the whispers among the curious villagers went quiet as all eyes moved to the priest, who gracefully ascended the platform and stood and addressed the villagers.

'A wolf is no less a wolf because he drapes himself in sheepskin and befriends the sheep and receives the sheep's kindnesses and does as the sheep do. He keeps secret his designs for the sheep, and the Lord tells us that if care is not taken His flock are to be food for the wolf.'

Congregants placed items before the villagers for all to see. Among these were various stolen goods, a ledger that detailed many village names and the items stolen from each, parchment containing lines and responses to be memorized that describe devastation by giant or earthquake or monsoon or revolt, and drawings that illustrate efficient plans of theft. 'You have stolen from the Lord and, it appears, from many others.'

'Those are not ours. We have not seen those before,' the elderly man said. The other refugees echoed his words.

'Lies are transparent before the Lord.'

'Very well, they were lent to us.'

'Avert your ears. The wolves have tongues like the Morningstar.'

'We have tongues as men and women do!'

Congregants stacked wood beneath the platform and formed large pillars and returned moments later with lit torches and awaited further command.

'Confess your treachery or burn, one and all.'

The boy tugged the shirt of the villager beside him and said, 'Someone must stop this!' The villager ignored his repeated warnings.

The elderly man cast his gaze over the villagers and said, 'At least one among you surely sees the madness in such a threat!'

None among the crowd expressed their concern, and in the absence of condemnation, the boy raised his disapproval but was drowned out by the villagers who had climbed back onto the wagon and made louder their solicitation for the refugees to burn to ash.

'Will you set us aflame if the truth is given?' the elderly man said.

'I will allow the Lord His judgment.'

The refugees urged the elderly man to silence, but he hushed them and said to the priest and the villagers, 'Our village did not suffer destruction at the hands of a giant. There is no village. There is no giant.'

'No giant?' the priest said. He clasped his mouth and clutched the cross draped around his neck.

'No giant?' The villagers repeated his exclaim.

The elderly man continued, 'Our performance misled you. Most of those who stare down upon you, myself among them, have not a home. We, each of us, left behind many horrors and joined as one people. We are wanderers. The minor injuries you remedied were self-induced in most cases; the more serious were applied by others. We find it disarms suspicion with rapid effect. Some have become quite adept at the manufacture of wounds. The process is as thus: we enter a village under the guise of distress and are welcomed. We are fed. We are given beds and soft linen. We are tended. We rest. We observe habits and items of value. We strategize. We thieve unnoticed. We leave under cover of night and enter the next village to begin again. We have only one another. We are family. We have survived in this way.'

Not a sound left the priest or the villagers or the boy. Each and every one was frozen with faces locked in states of shock.

The priest approached the children among them.

'You have thrust children into your scheme, vile sinners!'

'Those are not children,' the elderly man said.

Upon closer inspection, the priest announced to the village, 'These are no children, indeed, but little men and women.' The little men and women cast insults at the priest who spit at his feet and gathered the hems of his robes and hurried off the platform. One villager ended the disquiet with cheers for the refugees to burn; others joined in.

The priest silenced them and recited to the bound refugees, 'Unscrupulous conmen will exploit thy faith. They are as deceived as the people they lead astray. As long as they live, the world will worsen.'

'But you will leave Him to judge us, yes? Yes?'

From a congregant the priest took a lit torch and stood nearer the pyre. Flame light danced upon his wild eyes and he said, 'Then I saw a great white throne and Him who was seated on it. Earth and sky fled away, and no place was found for them. And I saw the dead, great and small, standing before the throne, and books were opened. Then another was opened, and it was the book of life. And the dead were judged by what was written in the books in accord with what they had done. And the sea gave up the dead who were in it, Death and Hades gave up the dead who were in them, and they were judged, each one of them, in accord with what they had done. Then Death and Hades were thrown into the lake of fire. This is the second death, the lake of fire, and if anyone's name was not found written in the book of life, he was thrown into the lake of fire to burn.'

The elderly man said, 'You may unbind us now so that we may live our lives with this shame and perhaps repent and perhaps receive the Lord just as prescribed. We can forget this mess altogether, yes?'

'And a fire blazed up their company. The flame consumed the wicked.'

The elderly man, the refugees, the villagers, and the boy witnessed the priest lower the torch upon the pyre and the ravenous spread of fire that followed. The dead wood was eager to ignite. Tall flames devoured the platform with haste and greed. The villagers applauded and hurrahed and sang hymns with the choir and overcame the refugees' screams with praises for the Lord.

'Will no one stop this?' the boy shouted, but none listened. He meant to hurry the wagon back to the traveler, but more and more villagers piled on for an uninterrupted view of the horror, and the escalated weight prevented him. 'Get off!' the boy cried, but they did not. The villagers continued to pile on until a wheel snapped in two and the wagon tipped and dumped them onto one another in the mud. They rose and laughed and scattered like mice. The boy turned his back to the roar of the fire; he could not bear to watch any further. He did not see the faces of the refugees but instead those of his mother and father and sister. He towed the broken wagon to the guard post against the agony in his back, and he cried as he did. His tears did not cease when he crumbled before the traveler, they did not cease when the traveler accosted him with questions about the wagon he was sent for, they did not cease when the traveler discovered the broken wagon that waited outside which he proclaimed in its current state was of no use to him, and they did not cease when the traveler demanded he cease his tears.

The boy's tears ceased only when he noticed traces of the apothecary's herb on the traveler's nose and lip, then a series of knocks rattled the door. The traveler asked the boy what was wrong, what was he looking at, then opened the door to find watchmen and congregants in wait and with shackles at the ready.

The priest entered and said, 'Please accompany us.'

The traveler gauged each exit and raced for the furthest one where, on the other side, he collided with more congregants and more watchmen.

The traveler shifted his disposition and tested the door.

'Yes, it appears in working order. Apologies. You were saying?'

'We have questions. About the giant.'

'We will answer here. The boy was moments from making coffee. Weren't you, boy?'

The boy wiped his tears with his dirty sleeve but otherwise stayed quiet.

'I prefer answers in the house of the Lord.'

The watchmen descended on the traveler and shackled him without resistance.

'What foolishness you will feel when you learn of this most assured misunderstanding.'

They dragged the traveler outside where a thick pillar of dark smoke towered above the village.

He said, 'What is that smell on the air?'

'The boy, too,' the priest said.

The boy was shackled next, but he kicked and twisted, and the watchmen struggled to detain him. One strong club to the back crippled him with pain, and he was made pliable and marched alongside the traveler to the belly of the church, where they were placed behind iron bars and locked away. The boy sat in the corner furthest from the traveler, where it was dark and cold and wet, and suffered a current of pity and loathing and deficiency and loneliness and disdain, which he aimed upon himself and which brought him to sobs and clenched fists and the desire to hit and hurt. He could not lie flat, his back pain prevented him, and he cursed the traveler for being tasked with retrieving the wagon. Hours passed. Moonlight entered the cell through a hole in the stone wall. Plump and curious rats came and assessed the boy and the traveler and then skittered deeper into the church.

The boy's inward battle left him hollow and tired and frozen beneath his skin.

The traveler interrupted the quiet the boy had welcomed to say, 'So, any ideas?'

CHAPTER TWELVE

Morning came and neither the boy nor the traveler slept longer than a moment. The boy's body wanted sleep but he was unable to grant it; his mind was broken and could not settle into such a peaceful state.

They were not fed or given water.

The traveler made attempts to speak with the boy but was met with silence, which only encouraged the traveler into further one-sided discussions that went in circles again and again.

Outside, dismissed volunteer guardsmen protested the traveler's imprisonment.

Sounds of their protest whispered through the thick walls of the cell.

'Was there ever a giant?' the boy said.

The traveler quit his discussions and said no more.

On the second day, the traveler offered a bribe to a devout congregant for a grant of freedom for him and the boy, who wanted no part. The congregant dismissed him with quotes from the Good Book and promised to pray for the traveler's soul and pray that he might one day know his second body in paradise, surrounded by family and loved ones for all eternity, amen.

'Eternity with family? This cell is preferable, thank you.'

'And deserved,' the boy said.

'No crime was committed.'

'Was the intention not to consolidate the village's wealth? Was the intention not to cart it away and leave this town to rot in poverty? And was the intention not delayed because, by happenstance, yet another party sought the same ends? How many villages have you taken to ruin?'

'You think me a conman? You think me cut from the same cloth as those poor souls?'

'I think you disgusting. I think the devil himself would be victim to your mastery of deceit.'

'At least you're talking to me.'

'My words contain truth. Yours are empty, and I wish not to listen to them.'

'You have listened, and you have listened well. You have been difficult, but you have done all I have asked, even when it was uncomfortable, even when the request was illogical, and even when I gave no explanation or evidence. You came to depend on my favor. All I simply had to do was pay attention to you when all others rode past you, when all others left you behind on the empty road you accompanied me because I stopped. I dare you to disagree.'

'I was to starve? You say a giant comes. I was compelled.'

'The good people of this village banded together to face one mounting threat. A purpose was presented to them. For one blissful moment, this village was inspired and cooperative. They understood their lives could be lost to this threat but still freely offered them for a greater good. Does that mean no less if the threat does not exist?'

'Is that how you justify your pilferage?'

'Not all claims I made were false.'

'Just the ones of consequence,' the boy said.

The traveler strode across the cell and drew back as if to hit the boy but went still when the boy did not shy from his swift approach. The traveler looked away in shame. He released his tension and after a moment sat by the boy in the dark and cold and wet corner. The boy scooted away, and the traveler followed, but the boy moved again, further. They repeated this several times, and the boy was first to give up.

The traveler said, 'A giant did destroy my village when I was no older than you; that was spoken true.

116

It did spare me and only me. I spent much time in an attempt to understand why, and I have found I cannot, if a reason exists at all. I also spoke true that our paths did cross again. I was not yet a man. I meant to confront the creature with my anger. I was afraid, and I fled. I have not seen it since, and I have not sought it out. But I have tamed my fear. I wield it.'

'No, all you have done is pass it to others for the purpose of enrichment, and it has spread like a plague through this village, and it has roused a wickedness I have seen too many times and one I cannot bear any more.'

'My venture has never before gone into such a dark manner.'

'I've no doubt if the refugees could, they'd make a similar commentary.' The traveler had no response to give the boy, so he moved to the other end of the cell. The boy offered one more question and then went silent. He said, 'If the giant did come, would you stand against it?'

Molded bread and well water were brought. The boy ate and drank quickly, so as not to taste its foulness. Sediment in the water stuck in his throat, and he coughed up dirt. The traveler left his plate untouched. Rats stole the bread.

On the morning of the third day, the boy was woken and brought into the priest's chamber within the height of the church tower. An agreeable view looked down upon the village and upon the pile of wood and ash that was once the platform, and upon the protest, which grew by the moment. The priest was listening to them shout and recite chants by the window when the boy was shuffled in and forced to sit at a large oak table filled with breakfast meats and cakes and pies and candies.

The baker, who had delivered and dressed the table, took his leave.

'They tell me the elder will recover but has been made cripple by his wound.'

'I'll shed many tears,' the boy said.

'He has much fear and paranoia and has turned the village hall into a fortress. He has empowered me to conduct village affairs. I have often said the church knows best.'

'I would disagree if I were not your prisoner.'

The priest gestured to the diverse spread and said, 'Sample in part, or in whole, anything which might catch your eye or please your tongue.'

The boy searched the table over from where he sat, then slid a platter of fruit-filled tarts off the edge, and he did so without interruption of eye contact with the priest. A clang echoed about the chamber and tart and cream and fruit splattered along the stone floor.

'Excellent, straight to questions then,' the priest said.

'You'll have no answers from me.'

The priest served himself cake then sat opposite the boy and ate. Each bite was accompanied with an overly produced smack of his lips and tongue.

'Are you familiar with the notion of a prophet?'

'Only the false ones.'

'I am authentic. I have proof, I have testimony, I have witnesses.'

'Produce it then.'

'I prophesied the short summer and the long winter and the death of the crops, I prophesied the dramatic regrowth that followed.'

'You saw the changing seasons. Groundbreaking.'

'The Lord converses with me. He makes known His will to me.' The priest shoveled more cake into his mouth and chewed and spoke at once. 'Target me with your fury for my actions if it pleases you, but know that I am but an instrument. Resentment upon me is, too, resentment upon Him, and the conclusion of that path is known to both of us, is it not?' The priest sucked down a glass of milk that dribbled down his chin, which he wiped with his robes.

'Men such as you always speak your filth and spread your hate and you hurt the other, then cower behind your book to evade reprisal. A more pathetic sleight does not come to mind.'

'The Lord tells us to "Live such good lives among the savages that though they accuse you of doing wrong, they may see your good deeds and glorify me".'

'The Lord must be quite pleased with you.'

The priest threw his plate against the wall, where it shattered to pieces and caused the boy to stiffen in his chair, and the priest shouted, 'The faithful are at war!'

'Show me the battlefields filled with corpses of the faithful, and I will rebuke all I have said in an instant.'

'I cannot. It is a war of morals. The casualties are the souls, the theater of battle is the Lord's nation, and I will listen not to those who say it does not belong to Him. We forfeit ground to women who seek to live without a man, we forfeit ground to sodomites, we forfeit ground to heretical faiths who seek a voice, we forfeit ground to the youthful ministries who read His words with a new and liberal appraisal, and we forfeit ground to those who would exploit His children. Man will be damned if such things prevail. The Lord gives me autonomy to wage His war as I see fit.'

'Return me to my cell at once. I'd rather listen to the traveler's nonsense.'

'Two paths now divide before you. One ends with unimpeded freedom and a forgiveness of all deception you took part in, whether known or unknown.'

'The other?'

'Holy fire.'

The boy allowed the priest his full attention and said, 'What will my freedom cost me?'

'Confess the traveler's maleficence before the village at sundown. Your admission would rescue those wrapped in falsehoods, and the Lord would praise your courage and welcome you to His bosom. Do this, then wander empty roads to your heart's content.'

'And the traveler's fate?'

A congregant entered to remove the boy.

'Deliberate on your choice,' the priest said. He took another plate and piled cake and pie and candies upon it.

The boy was thrown back in his cell where, to his surprise, the traveler was deep in meditation and recitation of the mantra the boy had taught him. The boy stood in the dark unnoticed and observed the waves of emotion the traveler endured behind his closed eyes and beneath his still form and upon his opened palms. Small tears formed in the boy's eyes, and he quickly wiped them away before they could be seen. The traveler emerged from his reflective state free of worry and with a smile. It was the first one the boy had seen from him.

'Is our freedom imminent?'

'It is.'

The traveler stood and swiped dirt from his clothes. He said, 'Wonderful. What else was discussed?'

The boy lay on the stone, faced to the wall, and said, 'I am tired.'

'Yes, rest now. We will leave this awful place upon our release, and we will not look back, and I do say we will happily forget these weeks. Won't we? What else, I've half a mind to request apology, too, from each of the leaders. But I suspect it would not be entertained. When we are free, let us make for the east. I've many questions and interest in the practice which you have learned me. Though it does thrill me, I've no wishes to scheme any longer. My ways are changed, boy. Does that please you?'

The sun set, and the cell filled with the pale of its orange and green and blue fire.

'Disappointment finds me wherever I lie,' the boy said. 'It spares none. My family surely felt it for me as they burned and I did not. Faith cannot be placed in any thing nor any man, it seems.'

The traveler kept the boy's words for some time. Then he said, 'If the giant did come this night, I would stand and fight.'

Congregants in robes appeared, followed by a pair of watchmen with swords.

The boy said nothing as they were asked out of the cell and escorted from the church.

CHAPTER THIRTEEN

Cold night approached and the whole of the village collected before the church and stood with torches and lanterns and appeared as a sea of warm and eager stars in the dusk.

The traveler and the boy were shepherded through the center and any deviation was corrected by their armed chaperons, and the villagers parted for them and stared and whispered and pointed. A thousand eyes watched their movements and the boy felt the urge to crawl out of his skin but kept his gaze to the ground and out of sight of the traveler.

'What is this? A farewell celebration?' the traveler whispered to the boy.

'Quiet,' the boy said.

'It's very thoughtful that they should send us off.'

'Quiet.'

'Did you arrange this?'

The traveler issued many thanks to villagers they passed for their attendance and shook their hands and explained the depths of his relief and excitement. An odor lingered among the men and women and children, and through the courtyard, which the boy found offensive.

The traveler whispered, 'The lack of soap and wash I will not miss.'

'Quiet!'

The last of the crowd separated, and before the boy and the traveler waited the priest and the head of the watchmen and two stakes that had been dug into the dirt. Dead wood had been piled around each base, and bindings were ready for use.

The priest wore a robe black as night and a golden cross around his neck. A dark executioner's hood covered the head of the watchman's face; a slit had been made near the mouth, and behind it was a smile.

'Oh,' the traveler said of the sights that awaited him. Without warning, he burst into a sprint. His path was swiftly blocked, and he was then taken to a stake but slipped free and again ran a short distance. He was tackled and returned to the stake and tightly bound while he pleaded for freedom. The boy watched all of this and said not a word. His head hung low, and he continued denial of eye contact with the traveler, even as he called to the boy.

Watchmen waited near the second stake, ready to bind the boy too, but the priest stayed them with his palm and approached the boy.

'You were given two choices.'

'I was given no choices,' the traveler interrupted.

'Have you made a decision?'

'I have,' the boy said. He looked to the traveler and saw the fear rampant in his eyes, then promptly twisted his focus away.

The traveler shouted across the platform, 'What arrangement have you come to?!'

He screamed it again and again until the head of the watchmen bound his mouth. It was not enough to mute him. He continued with muffled demands.

'My flock, the boy offers a confession to you. He means to cleanse his soul of the traveler's lecherous sewage, and we will hear him, and we will understand him, and we will forgive him, and we will be done with this emancipation of labor, emancipation of church, and we will be done with this entitled nonsense, and then we will worship in the Lord's house and we will tithe and we will return to our responsibilities, one and all.'

The priest shoved the boy forward, and all the eyes of the village settled upon him. A moment of contemplation occurred in which the boy surveyed those who stared at him and picked their noses and distracted themselves with hushed conversation and who had no investment in what was in front of them; the priest, who clasped his hands and shut his eyes and praised the Lord; the head of the watchmen, who struggled to light a torch until he removed his hood for improved visibility; the disgruntled workers and dismissed volunteer guardsmen, who yet held a spark in their eyes; and the traveler, who had not a look of betrayal or rage but of sadness and who wept in such a calm manner.

'Confess,' the priest said.

'I will not.'

A gasp spread. Whispers filled the air. The priest noted the arousal that took the villagers and caused them to waver, and he said, 'A moment, please.' He took the boy by the shirt. 'Have you the want for the Lord's anger? Have you the wish for the sloths and the prideful and the godless to thrive? Have you a desire to burn?'

The boy removed the priest's hand from his shirt, to which the priest took great offense, and assumed his place at the second stake, at the traveler's side, and there he waited to be bound. With the priest's acknowledgment, the head of the watchmen secured him to the stake. There was no slack; the tension kept the boy short of breath. He made great effort not to weep with some success. He held his head high and met no one's eyes. He looked at the night sky. He hoped the fire would swiftly end him, as it had his family.

With the priest's final acknowledgment, the head of the watchmen set first the traveler's pyre then the boy's aflame. There were no cheers from the village, only silence and observance. Not one villager turned away; all were locked on the boy and the traveler, save for the priest, who knelt and declared these offerings to the Lord. Sweat began to trickle down the boy's cheeks and he felt the moisture on his skin beneath his loose clothes. Below, the flame took and ate the pyre. The traveler's was further in its growth. Flame heated the fabric of the boy's trousers. Sweat ran down his legs and soaked his undergarments. The soles of the boy's shoes baked. The boy wanted it over and done, and he wanted it now.

Then a voice broke the disquiet. It came from the wall, from the small-headed man. He waved his hands, which held entry forms, and he said, 'Ho! Something does approach!' The large gates opened, and entered a riderless horse, then a second, and then a third. More entered; the hair was matted with blood, and these carried bloodied banners and the corpses of watchmen, some dragged them. The corpses were contorted in all manner of angles. Legs and limbs and torsos were broken and twisted and split. The boy recognized them as the brave watchmen who had ventured beyond the wall many days prior with claims to slay the giant. Of the few dozen, not one survivor rode in. The horses rushed the courtyard and dragged the mangled corpses past the villagers, the priest, the head of the watchmen, and the boy and the traveler, and a shudder made the ground squirm.

Homes and shops and trees and the boy's and the traveler's stakes and the church shook. Dust and loose wood and stone shivered and fell. Caged chickens and pigs screamed and fought for freedom; cage-free chickens and dogs and cats and cows fled the village. A second shudder caused villagers to stumble and fall and windows to shatter and the weakest of homes and shops to collapse and the contents of other homes to tip and shuffle. A third brought down roofs and sturdy homes and the church's tall tower, which crushed the villagers caught beneath. The crowd separated like insects. A fourth crumbled sections of the wall and set loose untamed fires anxious to devour the village. A fifth rattled the boy's and the traveler's stakes free from the earth and the burning pyres and rolled them to face the church and away from the wall and the havoc.

A sixth did not come; in its place was the quiet and the settling of the air and the ground and the crackling of widespread fire and the rush of feet and the cries and sobs and the prayers of the priest and the congregants, and then, from the dark above the village, fell a sound that resembled an animal, or a herd of animals, and it heated the air like lightning and shook it like rolling thunder. Dismissed volunteer guardsmen swarmed and freed the boy and the traveler, and the boy stood and caught full breaths, but his lungs seized when his eyes found the face that peered through the rising smoke that climbed into the sky. It released a roar, and the boy's bones rattled and his sight blurred and his hearing devolved to hums and buzzes.

When his hearing returned, the volunteers were yelling at the boy, and when his sight steadied, he watched, with arrest, the traveler flee the village with the rodents and the dogs and without a reverse look.

'We have readied for this day,' the dismissed volunteer guardsmen said.

They formed rank and were ready to heed the boy's instruction. Behind them a good distance, a flame towered and homes and shops lay in piles and villagers ran and advised desertion and a search for safety.

'What would you have us do?' they asked the boy.

Ruination surrounded them.

'We slay the goddamn giant!' the boy shouted, and he ordered the volunteer guard to man the wall defenses.

Two-man teams loaded the ballistae armaments across the wall and armed the skeins. Others gathered shields and swords and bows and arrows and prepared for battle. The boy stationed himself among the guardsmen on the wall. Before them was the black and shapeless valley. A rotten odor drifted down and climbed in the men's nostrils and stayed. Some vomited. Firelight raised and carved the giant's obese form out of the dark and the night. The wall was infantile under its immensity, and the men and the boy atop were but ants and were made to feel as such. The boy felt adrift in a foreign ocean and placed his palm on stone to hold himself steady.

The dismissed volunteer guardsman closest to the boy said, '"Do not fear its impossible proportions. Men, when acting as one, can best any foe." When I remember this, it does allay my quick heart and lessen the panic I hold for my wife and children.'

'Who has told you such bravery?'

'The traveler. Is he atop the wall? Perhaps further down?'

The boy lied and said, 'Yes, he is further down.'

'I am pleased to fight at his side.'

Another roar rained down on the wall and signaled the giant's rage, and the boy ordered the ballistae to aim and unleash their steel-tipped bolts. They did, and each one malfunctioned. The men who wielded them were cut in two by snapped torsion cords and impaled by misfired bolts and they screamed and blamed poor construction and the traveler's poor design and cried for help. They were answered by the giant's colossal and portly foot, which obliterated the defensive wall and threw the boy like a doll. He landed on hard earth and debris crushed him and pinned him and broke bones in his arm and leg. Awareness of his surroundings came and went and came again.

Dust from the wall caked his throat and nostrils and eyes, and each breath caused exquisite pain. His back and his fingers and toes were numb. The courtyard stretched before his limp body.

He lay helpless and watched the giant invade and the priest scurry into the church and lock out the fleeing congregants and villagers who beat on the church doors and cried for sanctuary. They were denied. The giant reached his fat hand in and plucked the priest out and bit him in two and chewed both bits to paste. The paste he spit upon the congregants before he stomped them dead. Watchmen dropped their weapons and retreated and shoved villagers in their path to the ground. The head of the watchmen stood before the giant, frozen with fear. Tremors shook him. The giant paused its violence to observe the small man and listen to his pleas and his begging. Gently the giant lifted him and held him to its eyes, and then it threw him across the valley.

The boy crawled from under the debris and lay in the street, and villagers fled around him; none stopped to help. The giant dropped both fists onto the village hall and it fell to pieces and sprinkled the coin and the jewels kept within across the courtyard. Coin and rings and jewels fell on the boy.

Villagers who stopped to collect the wealth around the boy were swallowed whole by the giant and it paid the boy no mind, it moved to other sections of the village and destroyed homes and shops and squeezed merchants until they popped like blisters, and soon the courtyard quieted. Distant screams and destruction washed the street, and the boy took his time getting on his feet. He hobbled on one foot; the other was bent in the wrong direction. He moved past the dead and the wreckage and offered them no mind and exited the village gate alongside others in peril. He followed a line of displaced villagers into the hills. None spoke; most wept.

Ahead of the boy, disgruntled workers had formed a checkpoint and were mugging at knifepoint any merchants or nobles found among the displaced. The noble before the boy refused to part with his assets and was forced to return to the village. They allowed the boy to pass, and he hobbled into the hills, where he lay in the grass and watched the giant rage against the structures and the people and he watched the fires empty the village and the dark smoke ascend and he listened to the screams that ripped the night and the pile of death that grew and he lay there, in the grass. He watched and listened.

He found a pouch among the launched debris and inside was the herb the traveler had concealed. He tasted it. It eased his nerves. He tried more.

Before morning, the giant tired and returned to the valley. The village burned through the day, until all was ash and scorched wood and piles of stone.

Groups of villagers returned and picked through the corpses and the shelled homes and pilfered what they could. The boy did not object but watched. By evening time, even they had gone, and the village was empty. The boy hobbled to the road. Smells of burning and death blew on the wind and followed him.

Travelers passed him and offered pity but did not stop.

CHAPTER FOURTEEN

The old man finished his warmed milk and took the boy's, though he had not finished, and limped to the kitchen. He stretched his stiff back and said, 'I crossed the traveler's path once more, several years later.'

'Did you scold his cowardice?'

'He was dead. I stopped to rest in a small village. His corpse had been hung at the gate as a warning to thieves and perjurers.' The old man drank a concoction of boiled herbs and butter, then stood as straight as his crooked back would allow. 'I buried him in a field and marked the land. I have forgotten where.'

'And what became of the giant?'

The old man led the boy into the back garden, which was enclosed by a private stone wall. A colorful flowerbed flourished and surrounded an immense skull, yellowed by rot and time. The jawbone had been wired open and wide. Inside the hollow of the cranium, a dining table and candleholders and a liquor cabinet had been placed. Remnants of an old dinner had been left on the tabletop and attracted flies.

'I was already a man when I found it and poisoned it while it slept. I can reenact its death thrall, if you wish?'

'Truly, you have lived through dark times.'

'It did not, at all times, feel as such.'

'But the horrors were plenty?'

The boy followed the old man to the front door.

'I do not disagree the horrors were potent in their moments and hours, and, yes, they did bring loss and tragedy to many, and thoughts did venture into despair and uncertainty, but each day had beauty somewhere within it, even the dark ones. Each day brought friends and fellow laborers and lively discussions on current happenings, like any other. Each day brought boredom too, and quiet and sleep, like any other. Each day united those who sought to court and love and marry, like any other. Each day families sat for dinner, like any other. Each day delivered moments of laughter and fun and surprise, like any other. Each day, women were made mothers and men fathers, like any other. Each day, seeds were planted and grew to trees and flowers, like any other, and each day, the farmer woke to tend his fields and his livestock, like any other, and each day had rain or storms or sun, like any other, and each day, children outgrew their toys and started work, like any other, and each day, old men and old women lived out their time and passed gently from this earth, like any other, and they did all this with horrors about the land.'

'I see.'

'You have heard my story.'

'Every word.'

The old man gave the package back to the boy and said, 'Then you have gathered why I will not now nor ever accept delivery of this package from you.'

The boy held the package in silence. He did not understand.

'I have wasted my breath. Good day.'

The door shut in the boy's face. Morning broke over the town. The boy returned the package to the supervisor without a word, then walked home. Usual greetings met him on the street, but the boy did not respond. He moved through the morning with his head down and did not lift it once. The apartment smelled sickly and ripe.

The boy's father held out his hand and said, 'Where are your earnings?'

'I have none.'

'You are here and not at work.'

'I do not feel well.'

'There is no coffee,' his father said. The boy made fresh coffee.

'Smells good, boy. I am to trial the factory today.'

'That was yesterday.'

'No, it is this day.'

'The factory will not have you,' the boy said. 'You drank and misplaced the day. My aunt said.'

'Your aunt is a cunt.'

'The factory will not have you.'

'There are others.'

'They won't have you either. There are no others. Do you not remember?'

His father sat on the couch in the stains where he had slept and poured brown liquid into his coffee. He said, 'That is my business.'

'And when rent is not made, it is mine, and when the table and cupboards and cooler are empty of food, it is mine, and when the winter lingers and we cannot warm the apartment and we get sick, it is mine, and when the boys play in the street while I work, it is mine, and when they go to school to learn and read books and study and I receive no tutor or literacy lessons and cannot surpass you in intelligence, it is mine.'

The boy's father slapped him and then slapped him again and shoved him to the floor and dumped coffee over the boy's head and rubbed it into his face.

'I am dependable; you have learned this from me. I am honest; you have learned this from me. I am your father, and you are grateful for it!' The boy's father filled a flask from a bottle. Before he left, he said, 'Tomorrow you work, and you will give me your earnings.'

The boy warmed water and bathed and lay in bed. The day ended. His father returned. His stumbles and his laughs and his songs were loud. The boy heard bottles open and glasses clink and glass smash and gross laughter.

At his opened window the boy stood. He leaned into the night and the cold and whistled for his aunt. It echoed. She would take him from this pit, she had said. The boy waited by the window. She would come. She had said. The boy waited. Late was the hour. Still the boy waited. He whistled again and waited.

She would come.

She had said.

CHAPTER FIFTEEN

The boy's father awoke. Bottles lay about him. The sun had been up for some time, it filled the room.

A headache prevented him from rising too quickly. He stood and coughed up a substance that burned and swallowed it back down. He smelled the air.

'Coffee smells good, boy.'

The End.

Thank you for reading!

Ready for more AJ Saxsma? Visit AJSaxsma.com for news and updates.

CPSIA information can be obtained
at www.ICGtesting.com
Printed in the USA
BVHW042205151122
652066BV00003B/45

9 798218 038120